FABLE MANNY

WHEN PEN MEETS PAPER

By Michael Angelo
2021

I S B N :
9 7 9 8 4 5 4 8 1 8 9 8 2

2 0 2 1

1

00

PROLOGUE

00

Prologue

"Manuel, come inside! Dinner is ready!" Manuel heard
his mother calling him inside for dinner. He looked over
at Cindy and shrugged his shoulders as if to say, "Oh
well, gotta go now." Cindy was Manuel's best friend from
his third-grade class, and they were neighbors. They
shared the same interests: drawing, playing catch, and
building mud castles. It was always hard to part ways,
but they hugged each other and said their goodbyes.
When Manuel walked inside his house, he was sad not to
be welcomed by anyone. However, he was used to this
and usually ate his meals alone. On the table, he saw
that his mother prepared spaghetti and meatballs. The
room was utterly silent as he sat at the table to eat his
dinner. After dinner, he followed his daily nighttime
routine, showered, changed into his pajamas, and
listened to music. Although his mother rarely checked in
on him, she expected Manuel to follow the pattern she
made for him.
Manuel was a well-behaved child who always followed
the rules. He rarely got into trouble at school and always
listened to his parents. Which was why he was conflicted
when Cindy approached him in class the next day and
said, "Manuel, I have a crush on you." He felt like his
parents would have been mad if he were to get a
girlfriend. So even though he liked Cindy, he told her
that they could only be friends. Because of this, she was
upset, and she did not talk to Manuel for what felt like
months.

Manuel felt awful. He could not focus all day at school because he was worried about Cindy and conflicted with his feelings. As Manuel walked home from school on his own, his thoughts began to distract him from the drizzling rain. He thought about Cindy, what it would be like to hold hands and kiss her. He felt guilty for his thoughts because he knew his parents would never allow him to have a girlfriend.

Manuel's thoughts were interrupted when he heard a girl yelling. He looked around and did not see anything at first, but then he saw a woman crying on the side of the road. She was on her back and hugging one of her legs to her chest. Close to her was a bike that looked like it smashed into something. Manuel immediately knew that she was injured, but he did not know what to do. At this point, it was pouring rain, but he stood there, shocked. It was not until a man came and helped the woman up. They must have been strangers because the man asked, "Ma'am, are you alright? Can I help you up?" It did not take long until the woman was in his car, and they were off to the hospital.

That night, Manuel was not thinking about Cindy, the incident at school, or what his parents would have thought of him. The only thing on his mind was the helpless woman who fell off her bike. If it were not for the man to help her, she would have been in big trouble. That was when Manuel promised himself that his life goal was to help women stuck and needed assistance. He aspired to be just like the man he witnessed earlier that day which assisted the helpless woman.

01

CHAPTER

ALMOST HAD
ME

Fable Manny was not born in a dump. He was born in a home, an exquisite home right along the river in Mystic, Connecticut. His house was about a five-minute walk from the historic downtown bascule bridge, the centerpiece of this storied town. In addition, he had regular parents, a mother and a father, or so he thought. Manny was an only child that never went without. He attended prestigious private schools, as his parents valued education. Unlike most homes in his neighborhood, Manny had a collection of books he would read cover to cover. Reading expanded his vocabulary, piqued his curiosity, and took Manny places he had never been before, enhancing his imagination.

The home was a historic yellow Victorian with four bedrooms, two bathrooms, a kitchen, and a parlor. The house was built in the late 1700s by a sea captain that featured a widow's watch, allowing his wife a beautiful view of the Atlantic Ocean, and hopefully, their husband's return home from the sea. Manny often escaped to this railed rooftop platform to read his books and let his imagination run wild as a child.

He was not born with the name Fable Manny. He came into the world named Manuel Aponte.

Everything flipped upside down when his parents, chemists at Pfizer pharmaceutical, were arrested and imprisoned for creating and pushing a high-powered modern-day ecstasy that they called the MESS; his life changed, and so did his name.

Everybody who knows Manny knew that he grew up in Mystic and wound up on Staten Island with his Abuela, but how could he continue living a prosperous life. His Abuela did not work, collected social security, and received a small retirement check. They lived in a two-bedroom condominium in a retirement community. However, things did not add up. Manny continued to wear the illest clothing, drove a luxurious Mercedes Benz convertible, and attended the top prep school. After graduating, he attended the prestigious Yale University, where he earned his Ph.D. in Clinical Psychology. Manny paid cash for everything, even without a job, resembling the modern-day pimp. Nevertheless, he did not have an Abel Magwitch lurking in the shadows. He started his enterprise. He wisely invested his parent's fortune from MESS into stocks and flipped it to live the life of Riley while his parents were serving a 30-year bid.

~ Manny's POV~

Growing up, I vividly recall the conversations between my parents. They wanted me to grow up and be a worthwhile contributing member of society that helped others to the best of my knowledge.

They taught me the difference between right and wrong, prepared me to make the correct decisions, and emphasized a strong work ethic. Even though they fucked up getting their asses locked up, I believe they provided me with a rock-solid foundation along with my Abuela and the actual value of family. And for that, I will forever be thankful.

Twelve years later, it is a Friday at 9:30 PM, and I just finished another week of work in Manhattan. I have my private practice, and my parents would be as proud as fuck, because I live largely. I live on the eleventh floor in a dope penthouse in Tribeca, 91 Leonard Street, to be exact, in the city that never sleeps. I know many cats who had similarly lost their parents growing up and did not turn out too well, saying that I am among the lucky ones. What up, do-ers? My name is Manuel Aponte, but most of you know me as Fable Manny. I have traveled worldwide, dined at the best spots, sailed the seven seas, and kicked it with the most beautiful women. Nevertheless, the journey it took for me to get here was not easy. Some would say it was a miracle, but I call it fate. Let me take you back to the very beginning, where it all started. After my parents went to prison, I spent my teenage years in Park Hill, Staten Island, New York.

On the other hand, as Wutang called it, the Shaolin land. Growing up on Staten Island, life was not easy. Park Hill was crazy as fuck. Shattered beer and wine bottles covered the sidewalks and streets along with garbage, hypodermic needles, and human waste.

The neighborhood dope dealers and narcotic kingpins were flopped up, slinging rocks, while young girls played double Dutch and boys played basketball. It felt like someone had packed us in like sardines, in this place we called home or like the slave ships of our ancestors that were brought to this unstable paradigm.

Yet somehow, I saw the opportunity to make this place better and to make my pockets fatter. You see, where I came from, we had not been given any handouts. We had to survive, and to do that, you had to grind, and so I did. I was born three years after Roe vs. Wade passed. Can you believe that? I come from a long line of fighters, champions, and healers. My grandmother, who was every essence of a strong Puerto Rican woman, raised me. It was not easy, and she worked hard to ensure that I was taken care of. Tensions were hot, but things were dying down in the concrete jungle of New York, the belly of the beast. Some cats made it out, while thousands fought hard to make a living.

Even though I thought school was instrumental for a successful life, I fucking hated it. Not because I did not want to learn, but I felt the teachers did not care. Most were old, overworked, underpaid, or burnt out. I thought that I did not have the discipline, the teachers sucked, the lunch food was awful, and the rules were tight. School never came easy to me, so I spent more time fucking around than earning an education. Once high school began, kicking it with the honeys and writing lyrics became priority number one, as niggas started to call me "Manny A."

The cats and shorty's craved my lyrics as I spit vicious bars on the regular, demonstrating that music understood me more than education. Once I wrote my first lyrics, it was a wrap.

Even though I loved to spit bars, I realized that school was not going to be my vehicle to a career, and I envisioned a life filled with a level of happiness and satisfaction. Therefore, I said to myself, "There is no motherfucking way. I am working a dead-end job and living in Park Hill the rest of my life." Music was an integral part of my life, but it was not putting a scratch in my pocket, so pushing crack became my hustle, ending my education.

I started to get into hip hop after hearing some cats from Hollis, Queens, New York, Run DMC, drop "Hard Times," which echoed my lifestyle. When I listened to that song blaring from a giant boom box, I wanted more on the street corner from some OG nigga with a high-top fade. Kids were breakdancing in the streets on a piece of cardboard, surrounded by a wild crowd of onlookers, ushering in a new wave of music. Therefore, hip-hop became a vehicle for my creative mind to achieve the unachievable, demonstrating the oppressed soul has no boundaries. I was immediately inspired by hip-hop and culture itself and the early contributions of Run DMC, LL Cool J, MC Shan, and Big Daddy Kane.

Growing up in Park Hill, an environment designed to see the oppressed fail, hip-hop provided an outlet for me to express my pain and suffering through beats, lyrics, rhythm, and soul that echoed off the earth's atmosphere.

My boys Pancho and Tito grew up in Park Hill. We began to spit some dope verses, and Pancho became the illest beatboxer. When we combined his magnificent beat and smooth flow with our lyrics, we established our street credibility. However, pushing crack in Park Hill became my number one priority. I started dealing some giant cookies with my niggaz, moving upwards of $10,000 of product a day while putting $2000 in my pocket. As a 15-year-old young man, I loved the street hustler life and was earning some serious cream. We had the perfect system as we cornered Park Hill. Pancho stood outside, Tito patrolled across the street, and I pushed in the hallway of a dilapidated building. After a few hours, we could pull in 20 c-notes without breaking a sweat. However, we didn't have much of a savings plan because we pissed away our scratch by renting nice cars, buying the most fly clothes, shopping sprees in Coney Island, picking up honeys, and smoking weed. My decision-making was terrible, but the money was flowing.

After grinding and hustling all day, we worked on music at night. I did not want to push crack forever but needed to make a living. My goal was to make groundbreaking dope records and rapidly become one of the greatest rappers of all time.

Now that the Golden Era of hip-hop ended, hip-hop craved new blood that would usher in a new era, and I wanted to be an integral part of the proverbial "changing of the guard."

The stars aligned one evening in 1991 at Club Red in Staten Island. This dope atmosphere mirrored the setting in Eminem's movie, 8 Mile. The filled to the capacity crowd of 300 was electric as they anticipated a rap battle between some serious sword swingers. Many cats hit the stage and got the crowd bumping with unmatched unique style and flow.

Nevertheless, the decibels reached an entirely new level when these street niggaz, The Flop House, ripped the stage, gaining severe credibility. It was a matter of time before them niggaz blew the fuck up. Before they came out, I felt a massive wave of anticipation sweep across the packed crowd. Niggaz stood up, raised their arms as the background music faded down, and the lights suddenly went out into total darkness, clamoring to see these cool muthafuckers rip the stage. But when the stage lit up, and they performed, my adrenaline skyrocketed, and ideas raced through my head, envisioning a collaboration. It was evident they won over the crowd because them niggaz ripped it, but that was about to change.

After a quick convo with the club promoter, Staten Island was about to witness the baptism of Fable Manny. I came to Club Red that evening to be a spectator, but Pancho got me all gassed up and encouraged me to hit the stage. However, I had my work cut out because FOI was a tough act to follow, and they already had the crowd buzzing.

I grabbed a mic, feeling the rough texture on the palm of my hand, and busted onto the stage with reckless abandon. A smell of marijuana lingered in the air. A gentle breeze from the motion of the crowd soothed the sweat pouring down my face from the radiant stage lights. I glanced at the vibrant group and felt 300 sets of eyes glaring in my direction. This was a make-or-break moment, and it was evident I had to bring it.

When the beat dropped, and I began to spit bars, the packed, restless crowd swelled with enthusiasm. The intensity from the audience provided me with an extra boost of energy, as I became the living embodiment of the music that I worked so hard to create. My positive vibe was so electric that it could give a lifeless room a fantastic experience to be remembered. The shadow of negativity from pushing smack was secondary as I jumped at the chance to entertain with reckless abandon. When all was said and done, the crowd voted for the victor through applause, and I was crowned the champion.

Nothing could hold back my enthusiasm as I took down some official sword swingers, similar to cutting down the net at the Final Four. It was an honor to compete with this level of competition and receive love and respect from my new fans.

I could hear the tremendous buzz throughout the crowd as niggaz knew I was about to blow the fuck up. Overflowing with ideas and motivation, Manny Aponte was about to change the landscape and make an imprint in the music industry. I took my craft seriously and challenged my niggaz to create music never heard before. This was our window of opportunity, and we needed to take advantage of shit before it closed forever. The feeling seemed surreal because I was destined for greatness until my luck ran out.

It was a swelteringly hot afternoon in the summer of 1992, and Staten Island was in the middle of a sizzling heatwave. I rested a small white damp towel over my shoulder to wipe the beads of sweat off my forehead. I was on the first floor of a trap house that resembled an abandoned, dilapidated dwelling, sorting through my c-notes and getting products ready for the tweakers. It was tranquil after a steady stream of morning traffic. The quietness grew more profound, and I could hear the steady rhythm from my heartbeat as I looked to make my next move with caution.

I sat down on a rusted metal chair and placed $2,600 in the middle of a card table, and secured 15 crack rocks in the palm of my hand when I heard a thundering boom vibrate throughout the room.

A swarm of Five-O's kicked the door off the hinges, lunged in my direction, and slammed me face-first into the hardwood floor. Ignoring the pain in my face, adrenaline flew through me as I attempted to dispose of the crack. However, the officers pinned me to the ground without hesitation, and three large German Shepherds aggressively roamed the room and incessantly barked. I had nowhere to turn, and my drug empire had crumbled. While pinned to the floor, an officer frisked me for contraband and confiscated the rocks. The following words he uttered were, "You have the right to remain silent...," and I tuned out the rest. My hands were placed behind my back, and I assumed the position as I became arrested. The officer tightly applied the rigid handcuffs to my wrists, restricting my mobility. I squirmed a bit but felt the cuffs fasten tighter and tighter, so I remained still. A couple of officers lifted me off the ground by my biceps and stood me on my feet, and began to escort me out the front door of the trap house. Many thoughts raced through my head. I was shocked, frightened, horrified, and wholly shaken to the core.

The cops were not friendly, approachable, or talkative, as they appeared serious and all about business. It was apparent they would not give me an ounce of sympathy because I was a criminal and chose to be a dealer instead of earning money at a regular nine-to-five job.

As we exited the trap house, hundreds of spectators flocked to the area with curiosity, witnessing a defeated man's freedom end. I knew I was fucked.

In 1992, I began a two-year waiting game while I fought my case, spending time in the New York prison system and most of my time at Beacon, Brooklyn House, Oneida, and Rikers Island. Massive razor wire-topped gates at each prison reinforced my freedom was gone. My days of making music, grinding with shorties, and pushing crack were past tense, and I had to acclimate to the less-than-human conditions. Not only was chow disgusting, but also the living conditions were deplorable. I was confined to an 8 x 6-foot cage that included a metal bed tray bolted to the wall with a paper-thin mattress covered by an itchy wool blanket, a metal sink, and toilet, and usually one or two cellies. Gang life was no joke, like the Bloods, Crips, and Latin Kings intimidated inmates and recruited regularly, but I kept my distance and wanted no part of that life. In the past, I heard cats in the street talking about the glory of prison life and earning street credibility, but that is a bunch of bullshit.

I felt like the dumb ass behind bars in prison while people strived to meet their goals in society and enjoyed their freedom. To pass the time, I wrote lyrics, smoked weed, completed my chores, and hustled for commissary, and read psychology and sociology books.

I adopted the mindset not to get too comfortable, not wanting to be in prison forever, to get back on track to reach my destiny. I felt like the dumb ass behind bars in prison while people strived to meet their goals in society and enjoyed their freedom. To pass the time, I wrote lyrics, smoked weed, completed my chores, and hustled for commissary, and read psychology and sociology books. I adopted the mindset not to get too comfortable, not wanting to be in prison forever, to get back on track to reach my destiny.

Being in prison was a vicious blow to my soul. In the darkest of times, I became bitter towards the world and doubted that tomorrow was not promised and yesterday was gone. While struggling through my incarceration, I turned to God in the face of adversity and learned to appreciate each moment. I was able to accept personal responsibility for the crime I committed, cope better with the pressures of prison with God playing an active role in my life, and felt a sense of inner peace. As I found myself alone in prison, my belief in God strengthened, which kept me sane. We live in a fallen world, which does not reflect God's love and genuineness, and I was reconciling for my sins amid a two-year bid. So I prayed to God in search of strength to guide me through my trials and tribulations.

Word spread like wildfire throughout the penitentiary that I had been rapping with prominent hip-hop emcees, and cats were giving me serious props.

It was dope hearing cats gas me up, but it did not heal the pain inside as I wanted to be on tour and make shit happen. Instead, my ass was behind bars, preventing me from reaching my fullest potential in life. I had lost everything and wasn't free to do anything, leaving my mind filled with negativity in these bleak circumstances. During recreation, the road dogs, OG's, and goon squad watched MTV, and I wondered what could have been if I did not fuck up. But I decided never to look back. I was out of the picture, down in the dumps, felt sorry for myself, and had every reason to give up, but I made a life-changing decision. It was time for me to finish my bid, become mentally tough, take care of business, and get back to society, hoping someone would give me a chance. After 24 months, I got released from prison. All of my charges dropped because these dirty-ass cops arrested me and planted drugs in another case. As a result, my case was dropped since I never was convicted. With no criminal record, I was 18 years old with limited education and work experience. I salivated for an opportunity to get my life back on track but faced several obstacles to integrating back into society. Many ex-cons experienced economic and societal challenges preventing them from thriving, opening the door back up again to a life of crime. Still, that shit was not going to happen. I had already fucked up my life and wondered if my time had passed to live a successful life.

After suffering throughout my two-year bid, I stopped making excuses, adopted the right mindset, surrounded myself with positive people, put my faith in God, and allowed my new successes to energize me. When I went to prison, that threw a significant obstacle in my direction that I brought on myself, but I chose not to be enslaved by the disappointment. The idea of fucking up my life was a significant roadblock, but I never stopped trying and didn't allow myself to be defined by the impossible. I came from nothing and went through the storm, where I am; this is fate. I remained firm, kept my dreams alive, and learned anything is possible if you are willing to persevere and continue to strive for your destiny.

What up, do-ers? I am Manuel Aponte, but now you know me as Fable Manny.

02

CHAPTER

ONE MORE
TEST

Unfortunately, my dumbass still struggled a bit and had multiple brushes with the law. The outcome of these cases could have sealed my fate at an early age and prevented me from becoming Fable Manny. Fortunately, I could beat my chances and change the course of direction in my life to a more positive side. I dodged a huge bullet when I was accused of armed robbery. However, I was accused of robbing a train cart after sticking up a man with a cart and asking people for money and jewelry. I was facing a three to five-year sentence in jail if convicted. However, the case had no credible witnesses, and as a result, it got dismissed. Fortunately, I got given another chance. I was sweating bullets; that shit was about to get real, but I did not learn.

A few months later, I moved down to Norfolk, Virginia, to do a bit of dealing outside of New England. I hoped that a new territory would put all my problems behind me. However, some people were coming to my drug spot and trying to take over. In the drug game, you must control your territory, or you are out of the game. As a result, I shot one of the fools and got charged with attempted murder. This situation could genuinely have changed my life.

However, the case was dismissed because the man whom I had shot was now wanted for murder. This made him an unreliable witness. Damn, I was a lucky mutha-fucker.

This should have been a wake-up call for me since attempted murder could have locked me up in Virginia for twenty to thirty years. However, I still had not learned my lesson.

In addition to my significant charges, I had multiple gun and drug charges in Virginia, with intent to distribute. Unfortunately, I could not avoid jail time, and I was locked up for eighteen months and kept going back and forth to jail, but my charges were dropped again. When I got out of jail, the police knew me very well. I stood out well as I always showed them respect. I did nothing stupid like shooting in the air or running my mouth. The police knew if I did something, it was for a good reason, as someone tried to shoot me or rob me. So, for the most part, I showed the police a lot of respect. I never gave them a hard time or fought with them. I would run at times but never fought with them since they were doing their job. The irony to my relationship with the police in Virginia was years later, some of them would work the clubs as a detail when I was on tour. Therefore, I had no reason to hang my head around them since I always gave them respect.

There are different types of hustlers on the streets; some crave worldly possessions such as gold teeth, clothes, and sneakers.

All I wanted was bail and house money if I got myself in a little bit of trouble. I always found it necessary never to violate anyone, and as a result, I never had to look over my shoulder. Those that try to rip off people can never walk around and feel comfortable. I treated all people with respect, including my customers. I had a drug enterprise and made about $30,000 a day in Brooklyn dealing drugs. In Virginia, I had continued success and made about $25,000 a day. While in the new territory of Virginia, I continued to carry myself respectfully and stick to the code. The people who did not know how to carry themselves in Virginia left in boxes to return to New York City. I never wanted to be one of those people, so I always felt that being respectful as I worked the drug game was the right way to do things. I always thought it was essential to follow the principles of running a good business as a dealer. The first rule to any business is respect. If I treat others with respect, more than likely, I will receive it in return. The second and third rules are principles and loyalty. This is also what you do for yourself so that others will have this for you. If you cannot respect yourself, how can others show you respect? Many people went to jail because they were selfish, acted like followers, and looked for a shortcut. The dealers in the drug game that showed no loyalty were murdered, and those who took shortcuts ended up in jail.

I always stayed in line with the code of the street and kept myself safe. Today's people have no principles and morals, so things are falling apart in the game. Nobody listens; when the older people are around me, they will school me about something. I always found it essential to absorb their knowledge, listen to them, and take it all in. Entering the drug game for me was a no-brainer. I started to deal because my friend T, rest in peace, came home in a new Fila Suit with dope Run DMC Adidas. I asked him how he made money, and he told me it was by dealing. As I entered the game, I knew my grandmother would not tolerate a drug dealer in her home. If I stayed home, she would have busted my ass, which would have served me right. Therefore, I ran away from home, moved in with other drug dealers, and rented an apartment. Often I regret that my mother was not involved in my life. Every child should have their mother as an integral part of their development. If my mom was around, I might not have gotten into so much trouble; I would have been in some, but not to the magnitude I was bringing it to. I just really needed the balance that she could have provided. I always wanted to be like my father, who was a hard worker. He was a superman that did everything to assure we did not grow up in the projects. I was so fortunate to have benefitted from his excellent work ethic.

However, as I entered the drug game, I needed to move in a new direction.

As a teenager, I dropped out of school because my grandmother started looking for me at school. After I ran away from home, I continued to attend school. However, I decided to run the streets and piss through all of my dealing money. Instead of investing in property and apartments, I would shop every day, connect with older women, and get any materialistic possession I wanted. At the time, it seemed right, but using hindsight, I should have invested much more wisely. When I was in jail, I tried to deal a little weed for the commissary, as it was easy to get stuff in, and it would help me survive.

In my earlier years as a drug dealer, I remember many individuals influential to me as I started to enjoy hip-hop. Out of all the artists, Kool G Rap intrigued me the most. When I heard Kool G, it was as if he was speaking for and to me. I was living out what Kool G had to say. As I listened to his lyrics, it rang true to the life I was living. He spits a lot about what was going on in the streets and dealing drugs. This was a massive part of my life.

When NWA came through and jumped on the scene energetically, they gave me a boost with their energy and their attitude. I just knew that I was not alone after hearing their lyrics. These guys were making records on stuff I was doing.

This group out of Compton was no joke. They brought a new meaning to the game of hip-hop with their rough street style, and I loved it.

Eventually, I turned away from the drug game for good. I never turned back to it. I never had the urge to go back as I have no desire because people depended on me, and I would not want to risk losing everything. I lost many friends in the drug game, and it gave me many headaches. I was now intrigued by the possibility of making serious cash by going to college.

03

CHAPTER

MEET
ELIZABETH

Chapter 3 | Meet Elizabeth

Before going to college, I wanted to give music one more try. I began to work on my debut solo album, Meet Fable Manny. Throughout my career, I thought about a solo project. Unfortunately, time was never in essence. I spent the first twenty years of my life trying to find my way. Now it was my turn to go in a direction veered only by one captain, Fable Manny.

Ever since this hottie named Elizabeth bought me the appropriate equipment to record an album, I had plenty of tools in my studio, The Slam Factory, to make my album. My studio was located at the bottom of my duplex. It provided a pleasant atmosphere to reach my goals. However, I was in a dark place that did not permit me to release my album. As a result, it took two years to record and release Meet Fable Manny.

My life was filled with numerous obstacles that made it difficult for me to focus on music. As I recorded, I was in a long-term relationship that was going sour rapidly. I was unfortunate as I did not know how to get out of the relationship, and I felt stuck. It is sad when an artist cannot wait to hit the road to avoid the bullshit at home. That was my life with my ex-girlfriend, Elizabeth, at the time.

I would go out on tour for a month, and as soon as I returned home, the arguing would begin. At times, the moment I stepped foot on the parking lot of the airport.

The last day of the tour would always be a nightmare for me since I would be getting ready to go home. This showed a sign that my relationship was dysfunctional, but I continued to stay with her.

When I was at home, the relationship was quite toxic. She would interrupt a recording session for me to feed the dog or complete a menial task. I would go into the basement to record in the Slam Factory, and all I could hear was stomping on the floor from upstairs. It was so frustrating, and I wanted out. I felt trapped and did not know how to escape.

Fortunately, I had a friend who was an engineer from Worcester, Massachusetts. This was an excellent outlet for me as I did not know anyone and could get some things done. I went out to Worcester and recorded my album. My goal for this record was to bring everything together. It was eclectic, maybe even too diverse. I was very proud of this album. This was a very dark period in my life as I was getting lost in depression. I did nothing to support the record, no press, and only one show for the album. Being that I did not do too much press, it influenced the ability of the album. Sadly, my voice was lost in depression. It is like writing a book and just staring at a typewriter for weeks, and it remains blank.

Today it is difficult for me to listen to the album because of the bad memories. When I finally began to record, it had been so long that it took me a while to figure out how to get the equipment going. I was not feeling the music at all because it was a bad period. I was struggling with my girlfriend, and that affected my entire life.

However, looking back, I am proud that I was able to overcome those obstacles. All of my friends recognized that my relationship was toxic. However, they could not see that I was melting on the inside. I treated myself for depression at the time by self-medicating with weed and alcohol. I constantly wanted to stay above the clouds and not come down. Nevertheless, it did not work, and my music career began to unravel. The relationship was destructive in the way that I almost lost my friends.

An incident occurred with my girlfriend that put a strain on my work. She had befriended some of my boy's girlfriends. Her nonsense was affecting my relationship with them since we all toured and performed at the same shows. During one performance, this dude Simpson's girlfriend and Elizabeth got into a significant argument outback that almost came to blows. We were there to do a job, and the work environment was impacted negatively. Unfortunately, some people think it is all fun and games because we play music.

Nevertheless, it is our job, and if we do not perform, we are not paid.

Things got so bad that the tour manager called me before a show in Boston. I was performing with some real official hip-hop artists. There was a lot of thunder at this performance, and everyone wanted things to go right. To put into perspective how toxic my relationship was with Elizabeth, management made it crystal clear that she could not attend the performance. Immediately, I knew this would not go over well. She did not listen to me at all. In addition, it was her friend's birthday, and she had friends coming with her to the show. When I informed her about management's decision, she flipped. She said she wouldn't be told where she could go and was going no matter what. I just threw my hands in the air and gave in to her bullshit.

As I expected, my girlfriend went to the show anyway. She did not look at my profession as a job because of all the perks behind the scenes. However, people must look at our profession as work, and she could not see it. When the girls went backstage and drank free, they sometimes thought it was one big party. It especially was not cool when your girl acted like an ass at your job. Now she did not act up at this show, but she went. I had the final say, but I just let her have her way. I put my hands in the air since she was not listening, and she went anyway.

When she went, I was not hanging with the people, and it appeared as if I was doing my own thing.

When we flew back, the promoter came to me and said he wanted to give me a call "to talk." I have never been fired from any job, even when I had somewhat regular employment at a local music store. If I were to be fired, I had no plan B put in place.

I went to a meeting at the studio and sat down with the promoter and some of the artists. They had met before our meeting with me to decide how to deal with the situation. As an up and comer in the industry, I had no room to be a diva and did not need to bring bullshit to the show. I shouldn't be treated with kid gloves and needed to pull my shit together. In addition, Simpson did not want bullshit at home with his woman. If I could not control the problem, they would handle the problem, which meant I was off the tour.

It was decided that I was on a probation period. As a result, I wasn't allowed to do interviews, pictures, or any press at all at the shows. This would impact my ability to get my music moving. It was a blow to my ego, and I was devastated. The probationary period was about six months, and it was uncomfortable. This put me in a bad depression. These were my boys for years, and I was mad that I had allowed the situation to happen. I felt powerless, and that was the end of that relationship. After this consequence, the relationship ended.

I almost lost my job and had to worry about being viewed among my peers; it was a big problem. During that time, Simpson was the one that saved me. Despite all the bullshit, he did not give up on me.

Looking back, I understand their stance because it is a business, and you cannot allow something to fuck up your business. After about six months, my ex-girl was no longer coming to the shows, and she realized that she made a huge mistake. Little by little, Simpson divorced his ex-wife. He learned things were not my fault or even the fault of my ex. What my ex did wrong was not being respectful towards anybody. Simpson apologized for the whole bullshit, and I apologized to him. There was a definite strain for six months, but we got through it. However, I performed no matter what. I had been through worse things in the past, and I still went on to perform. Performing was my job, and nothing would stop me.

I never talked to relieve emotions, and everything had started to build up. I did not talk about my problems; I was young and never went to anyone. As a result, I did not have the correct coping mechanisms to deal with the issues that confronted me. The only way I dealt with things was going on the road to play and self-medicating. Being on the road was my escape from problems. I could have gone down the wrong path, but I was able to pull out. This was some severe abuse on my body.

When you do not have anyone on the road telling you "no," people give you whatever you want and support your habit. As a result, things never got better. They were so psyched to hang out with me but were not concerned about my well-being. The fans wanted to be on the stage, and I took advantage of what they brought. When I came back from tours, I would be a shell of myself due to all the partying. The stress of all of that wasn't working well during probation, but it eventually turned around.

When I listened to my solo album, I saw it as one of my missed opportunities. Had I did what I needed for that record, it would have been much better for me. Unfortunately, I was in a relationship that went longer than it should have been. By the time the relationship ended, I had no energy for anything, and it was time to make a change in my life.

04

CHAPTER

MY TIME TO
SHINE

As I embarked on my undergraduate education, I felt I
had to prove myself to everyone. After my parents were
no longer around, I was not under their blanket of
protection anymore. I had to do everything for myself.
This was not easy since people did not want to see me
reach the heights that I envisioned. It was my time to turn
into a man and establish myself.

It was a little frustrating as the grumbling could be heard
that I was not ready to make it big. While I was living
with my parents, nobody would put me down. My father
would not have tolerated such a notion. Now that he was
incarcerated, some doubters were starting to rise. Some of
the doubters were part of my old music team. At that
point, it was just a paycheck for them. When my dad was
around, I felt confident he could help steer me in the
right direction. It was not as if I had to start from scratch.
My father built a strong foundation. My goal was to keep
his momentum going and make the club owners happy. I
was concerned that the club owners would not be satisfied,
as they were the ones that hired the artists. Upon hearing
my father had passed, I was concerned they would drop
me from the clubs. With luck on my side, my father asked
them to give me a chance, and most of the owners
complied.

One person that allowed me to play in her club was Marla
Mable. She was a major actor who had a starring role on
one of my favorite television shows, The Gallagher's. This
was one of the biggest shows on TV at the time, and I
would always be watching the show.

I played at Marla's house a bunch of times when my
father was around. Marla was always really nice to me.
However, when my father was locked, she had a
significant decision to make. Marla could have easily
found another artist to play at her club. At first, she was
hesitant because it was a business.

Nevertheless, my father gave her a call one afternoon and
encouraged her to take a chance and let me fill in. She
gave me a chance. I played my heart out, and it allowed
me to keep on getting gigs. When my dad was
incarcerated, she let me play there for several months. I
was always grateful that she was one of the people that
gave me a chance.

A famous DJ, DJ Big Time, owned another club that gave
me a chance. His venue, Concerts on the Sunset, was
located in Manhattan. Big time gave me a chance to
perform, which led to multiple gigs. Since I killed it on
stage, it opened up the door for many other gigs since the
word spread that I was solid. To avoid too much change,
my rehearsals were quite similar to the way my father ran
things. I was doing some serious work as I began to prove
my doubters wrong.

After deciding to run in hip-hop for a year as a tribute to
my father, it helped me pay the bills and gave me some
pocket change.

If I was not looking at a star, I was looking at beautiful women. At the same time, I completed my undergraduate degree at Columbia University. I was getting an excellent education and having fun at the same time. I always thought it was dope that my friends from school would travel throughout New England to support me at my gigs. I must admit that it was quite the balancing act, but I love being a student by day and hip-hop artist by night. After a year, I had decided to take a break for about a year from the band.

After two years of the hip-hop hustle, I was a junior in college and had been performing to the point where record executives started to have an interest. I was contemplating whether I should sign a deal or go independent. After playing in the biggest clubs in New York, my name circulated as someone with promise as an artist. As a result, some calls were beginning to come in with great opportunities.

A great offer had come through to perform at the Playmate of the Year Party at the Playboy Mansion in Holmby Hills, Los Angeles, California. I had developed an association with Playboy because one of my boys from college was friends with Heff, and he took me to a jazz festival out there on one occasion. This led to my invitation to open up at a concert at the Playboy Mansion. It was the first time I went to perform there.

While playing at the Playboy Mansion, it was celebrities galore. If I was not looking at a star, I was looking at beautiful women. In addition, the famous Playboy Grotto had multiple beautiful women swimming around naked. This made me question the music game a bit. I saw all of these gorgeous women and began to put together a plan for being with multiple women and providing them with great opportunities.

The night we connected, I was so amazed that he was so humble and indicated that we would talk about future opportunities. We exchanged numbers and stayed in contact. This led to a fantastic call I received from him one evening. He was well-connected with this prominent actor, Shantel. He got a gig for me to perform at her birthday party. After the performance, Heff approached me and gave me some big props for my performance. I almost fell out of my chair when I received the call. I put down my phone for a second and pinched myself, believing that I was in the middle of a dream.

Shantel was more significant than life in Hollywood at that time. She had just completed her role as Princess Sherri in a colossal movie trilogy. As I was a big fan, I had watched all three movies, and there was not an individual throughout the country that didn't know her. Now I would be playing at her birthday party. My friends from school would never believe that Manuel Aponte was in this type of company performing.

However, it was reality, and I enjoyed every second of the ride. Simpson joined me at the party, which was located at Shantel's home in Beverly Hills. The mansion was set above the hills behind the Beverly Hills Hotel. This was a real Hollywood-style party. I had never been part of such an event as a performer. I vowed to put on the performance of my life and try not to be star-struck. Just as anyone would imagine, that would not be easy to do. I was pretty excited seeing these celebrities walk into the venue. While at the party, one of the first people I saw walk in was Rick James, as he walked in with his group, The Mary Jane Girls. At his side was his current girlfriend at the time, Catherine Bach. She was one of the hottest actors on TV that every male in the country lusted after. She played the character "Daisy Duke" on the hit Television series, The Dukes of Hazzard. Believe me; she was even hotter in person than on TV. Rick James was hysterical. As he walked into the house, he shouted out, "Where's the music at?"

In addition to Rick James and Steve Martin, Jack Nicholson sat about ten feet away from where I performed at the party. These two men were two of the most prominent male actors in Hollywood, and they were about to listen to my jam with my band. Jack Nicholson had been in multiple movies that I loved, and I was in the same room as him.

He was the lead actor in two of my all-time favorite film, The Shining and One Flew over the Cuckoo's Nest. In the same vicinity, Steve Martin was just as significant in Hollywood. Steve became well known for his recurring role on Saturday Night Live. He was the lead actor in the movie, The Jerk. Never could I have imagined playing in front of these two Hollywood moguls.

After the show, Shantel was cool with me. She was happy and having a good time. She was appreciative of my performance and gave me many props. I was paid very well for the implementation and left the mansion at about 3 A.M. Regarding Heff; I appreciated that he passed my name along to this party. This was a tremendous opportunity for me and just the beginning of my successful run.

After about a year, I started to bring some new blood into my act. We continued to play some of my music. However, we switched things up a little bit by playing some covers of other artists. We traveled the hip-hop circuit, and this added a much-needed newer flavor to the group.

At the same time, I was playing with other groups to keep my name out there and keep options open. One particular group I played with was MC 9, who back then went by Nine Lives. It was here that I met Puma, who was a dope producer and became influential to my career. He was the DJ and brains behind his group.

I was blown away when I found out that Puma went to middle school with my father. What a small world. As my music progressed, I asked Puma to do my production. Puma played the Conga drums, and I thought this would give a nice feel to my music, along with a DJ. Since the music climate had changed throughout the years, Puma embraced the opportunity to get back on stage and jam with me. It was great to have him come aboard.

Puma was hilarious. He was always talking about him and his boy Toby. It was as if Toby was his best friend. Initially, I did not understand whom he was talking about. After some time, I realized Toby was his prosthetic leg. Puma lost his leg during a tour in Vietnam. He added much-needed humor and became a great teacher to me. However, it was nice that he laughed about it and kept his great sense of humor.

We started to develop a great bond. I would go to his house, listen to music, his stories, jam, and smoke some weed. One day, I was at his home, and I noticed a drum that I had never seen before. He showed me an instrument that became a staple in his percussion setup. It was a drum called Djembe. This drum had a great look as it had goatskin and fur on it. As I tried to play the Djembe, I got slits on my fingers and could not play anything for about three days. Initially, I played it wrong, and my hands hurt.

What was more interesting was how Puma received this drum. In 1986, he went on a trip to Africa, playing with many of the hip-hop pioneers. Puma did a great job reminiscing with me.

One time I had a conversation with Buck that came back to me. He indicated that when he died, he wanted to die while playing. I thought that was crazy. I was slated to do the Bronx hip-hop Festival. We were rehearsing at Quad Studio in Manhattan. If you were a member, you could rehearse there in these fantastic rooms. Therefore, we rehearsed there for a couple of hours. As we went through one of the songs, we were playing and jamming pretty well. Since we were getting ready for the show, we stopped at a little less than 100%. As Puma began to solo on the Conga drums, he seemed to be playing a little weird. I did not know if he was joking or not. Suddenly, he stopped playing, fell backward, and started shaking before dying of a heart attack.

The music just stopped, and we stared at one another. Immediately, I yelled for help, but it was too late. Puma had passed away. I tried calling his girlfriend, but there was no answer. The following person I called was his brother, Boogie. He heard the panic in my voice and said he was on the way. I was in shock as I ran inside to tell the studio manager, who was in charge of booking the rooms, that we needed help. Those moments were a blur because of the shock, and everything was happening so fast.

Everyone loved Puma, and before you knew it, workers and people from the union came to our rehearsal room while Puma just laid there. I rode in the ambulance to the Hospital with Puma, and his brother met me. I did not rehearse at Quad Studio for a long time, and when I did, I never played again in the same room. This was hard because I had never experienced a significant loss in my life. Puma was not only a friend, but he had become a fatherly figure that shared many memories that my father would no longer be able to communicate. I miss Puma to this day and cherish my memories with him.

A couple of weeks went by, and Puma's girlfriend called me up and asked me to stop by the house. I went to the house, and she told me that Puma loved me and appreciated that I gave him another chance to play. This opportunity brought meaning to Puma's life again. Puma was passionate about music, and very few people hired or called him for gigs, and it almost destroyed him. The tide of music was changing with drum machines. It appeared that Puma and I were great for each other.

As I got ready to leave, Puma's girlfriend gave me his Djembe. She said that he would have wanted me to have the drum. I never played it, but it served as a tribute to him.

It was somewhat funny that I was not thinking about hip-hop at the time, but Puma gave me an integral instrument that I used to this day. This gives the 808 sound without using a machine. It feels great that Puma is still with me years after he has passed.

As my junior year of college commenced, it was time to enter my senior year of college. While at college, I continued to perform in the top clubs in New York City. I knew my way around, and all the players were on my side. I was able to go into a hip-hop club and get a weekly gig. I was able to sit in and play with many of the hip-hop legends. However, I started to get frustrated with my life and was a bit overwhelmed. I was 30 credits short of my degree. I was frustrated with the university. My gigs were tough to attend because I needed to graduate.

My frustrations spilled over, and I was out; I was over the edge. I had no one to speak to about the thoughts going through my head. I was jamming with my friends and doing gigs of my own with my peers. It was a big decision, and I did not want to disappoint anyone, but I knew what had to be done. I put music in the rearview mirror and put all of my focus into school.

My manager, Big Tony, was not particularly pleased that I decided to leave music. He understood the significance of my education and wanted me to finish since I was two semesters from graduating, but we were making big money on tour.

He made it clear that I needed to pick education or music. It took a lot of soul searching, but I wanted to be a psychologist, and music would only get in the way. As a result, I decided to leave the piece behind. I completed my last year of college in the blink of an eye, and four years later, I earned my Ph.D. in Clinical Psychology. It was time to start making bank, only this time without slinging drugs or making music.

05

CHAPTER

MEET PATRICIA

Shortly after I received my Ph.D. in Psychology, I started kicking it with the females. I was beginning to pop up on the radar screen with the shorties cuz they thought I was cute, intelligent, carried myself with confidence, and was in good shape. One of my homies told me that Patricia Mills was really into me the finest woman in Manhattan. Patricia was slamming, and I wanted to have sex with this dime.

How could I forget the first time Patricia caught my eye? I stood there outside in Times Square, mouth wide open, wordless, and sweating under the New York City sun. She had a thin waist, smooth chocolate skin, a big chest, and looked like a grown-ass woman. I was taken back that Patricia expressed interest, telling her friends I was a fly guy since she usually fell for thugs, gang bangers, and some OGs. Nevertheless, she approached me, and we started kicking it.

My courtship with Patricia was puppy love at its finest as we began to hold hands and share a kiss or two. Walking the block and getting props from the homies was fabulous because being with Patricia put me in a completely new stratosphere.

I felt my heart pitter-patter when we hung out and could not hold back my cheesy ass smile. We were kicking it for a few weeks when Patricia made it clear she wanted to fuck.

I knew Patricia was advanced, and I had minimal experience in bed, so I was anxious that I did not know what the fuck to do. However, it all culminated the night I popped my cherry.

One evening Patricia invited me to her crib for what I knew would be the night of my life. I had always envisioned my first sexual encounter, but I was now in the big leagues, and there was no turning back. I hopped in a cab and moved to her crib at light speed. When I knocked on the door, Patricia opened the door and looked as dope as fuck. I wanted to tear that ass up. She ushered me up the stairs and into her room, immediately locking the door in case someone stopped by.

Without hesitation, Patricia took charge and led the way. We sat on the bed, and she kissed me all over and began to take off my clothes. Patricia opened her dresser drawer and handed me a condom, and it was on; we had the most passionate sex on her bed, and I could hear Keith Sweat's Love Cuts playing in the background. It was evident that Patricia took charge, she was not a virgin, but it did not matter. She treated me like a king and the night was better than I ever could have imagined.

After sex, we kissed, and I felt unstoppable. This was the wildest night of my young life, one that would go down in the record books. My hands were shaking with excitement, and all I could think of was bragging to my homies about the fuck of the century.

For a second, I thought they would never believe me, but I could not believe my eyes. I was wearing a brand new black jacket with white lining splattered with some traces of blood because Patricia had her period. Even though I felt a bit grimy because she was on the rag, I knew that nobody could refute my experience when the dust settled. Therefore, whenever niggas said I never got laid, I displayed my white jacket with the red stain as my trophy. I kept that jacket for a minute.

Sex with Patricia was a transitional rite of passage because she was one of those shorties that knew all the older dudes. I was the cute baby-faced, sexually inexperienced psychiatrist, and she usually sought a drug dealer that could buy her whatever she wanted. I reflected on losing Patricia as a lover, which made me want to transition into manhood quicker.

Even though Patricia and I were a wrap, I got mad respect from the homies whenever I bragged about fucking her. This put me on an entirely new level, and I began to move up the pecking order. I had bitches looking in my direction that never gave me the time of day.

My brief romance with Patricia opened the door for me to step up my game with the shorties. For the most part, I preferred cute and sassy females with rigid bodies that stood out, like a model.

Occasionally, I hooked up with a quiet girl, but I kept it on the down-low. I was now as horny as fuck and began to chase shorties in Manhattan with confidence.

Fortunately for Manny, Patricia and he remained very tight. Patricia loved him enough, and their friendship was undeniable. She never got jealous or intimidated when Manny met new women, as she decided to become his partner. Just as Patricia helped Manny develop his confidence, Manny wanted to do the same for women and help them become wealthy and successful. Therefore, Patricia became a silent partner; one would even call a spy, which collected information on the women. Patricia was the key to his success. He moved to a luxurious penthouse in Manhattan to corner the market on rich women who desired to become famous. Manuel Aponte was now about to embark on his quest to become a gigolo and Fable Manny.

06

MEET LISA

One winter evening. I was out in Tribeca having a couple of beers with some colleagues when a beautiful blonde-haired woman caught my attention. Therefore. I watched her, seeing her reactions to everything around her in the chaotic environment. The bar was littered with drunks looking to get a quick piece of ass, and she respectfully declined many offers. She just had this confident and respectful way about her that made her so damn attractive. I hesitated to move in her direction, but I could not fend off the strength to be shy anymore. I made eye contact with her, navigated my way across the bar, and introduced myself to Lisa Close, a third-year Theater major at the prestigious New York University.

As I walked across the bar. I was unaware of my growing excitement; it could have knocked the wind out of me. Nevertheless. I gathered myself and let my confidence stand before me. letting Lisa know that I was worthy of her time. So there we were, the both of us, caught up in conversation, and everything around us stood still. Nothing else mattered as we had this real dope connection. Our conversation was so smooth, as if we had known each other for years.

I quickly became intrigued by her passion for becoming an actor.

She put in countless hours into her studies at NYU and made many sacrifices to follow her dreams. I listened as she whispered these words, "I may not be able to return next semester because I am unable to take out any more loans. I am concerned that I will never amount to anything."

Lisa was sober-minded and quite serious about her future. She worked long hours to put herself through NYU as a CNA, making minimum wage, at a local nursing home. Lisa carried herself quite maturely, resembling an older sibling, as she kept her eye towards a future on Broadway. Lisa had dark skin, a winning smile, and an athletic physique that replicated Venus Williams. She was born and raised in Yonkers, New York, with her eye on the big city of Manhattan to make it big. Lisa wanted to be the best actress to ever step on Broadway, constantly studying film, getting work done on her body, and taking dance classes. She practiced as hard as anyone, not wanting a substandard work ethic to prevent her from reaching her goals. Lisa had a brilliant theatrical mind and honestly felt nobody was better than she was. I found her level of confidence to be rather sexy.

A few moments later, we glanced at each other simultaneously. I knew by the look on her face that she was stressed mentioning her struggles.

However, it was as if the world had been lifted off her shoulders. I did not want to offend her in my response, but I wanted to know that I could assist. While I sat there in deep thought, there was second-hand smoke moving in our direction, so much that it began to bother me, but I swatted the smoke away. I had assumed that it was cigarette smoke since we were sitting in a bar, but the strange smell in the bar prompted Lisa and me to make a funny face. I could not believe some cat was smoking weed at the bar. I had not hit the pipe since college, but it caused me to reminisce.

As I refocused, Lisa and I talked about her struggles, but the sexual tension between us elevated and could not go unnoticed. While we threw back countless shots of tequila, Lisa began to undress me with her beautiful brown eyes. Before I knew it, we were back in my living room, having the most passionate sex one could imagine. We just had the dopest connection that I did not want the night to end. See, I know many dudes that would have fucked a hot shortie like Lisa and kicked her to the curb at the end, but that was not me. I wanted to see her succeed at the game of life and knew I could be her vehicle to success. Lisa was soft-spoken and quite intelligent. As we snuggled on my couch, we talked as if we had known each other for a lifetime.

We had a lot in common, and I envisioned her being one of my best friends moving forward. She had an easy-going personality that made it easy to kick back, relax, and talk freely. All of these traits made Fable Manny's wheels turn, knowing a solution for her struggles was on the horizon.

After a few hours passed, Lisa reached over and kissed me on the forehead. It was as if she assumed this was a one-night stand and I would never see her again. As she moved her head away, I could see the disappointment in her eyes. Nevertheless, that was all about to change. Several things could have happened at this moment, but I offered my support without second thoughts. Before I began to talk to Lisa, I overheard my neighbors yelling at each other in the distance. As I considered the possibilities, I put it all on the line. "How would you like your struggles to go away?" Lisa's head snapped up with a bit of suspicion but was filled with curiosity. It was evident that Lisa wanted her struggles to go away but did not know how. She had always worked hard to make her dreams come true and received very little support from her family. The fact that a stranger was willing to help makes no sense. Lisa probably thought I was buggin since I was drunk as fuck, or maybe she thought I was trying to get some more action. However, she had no clue that I could make things happen.

I looked out the window and noticed that the sun began to rise. The night flew by, and it was one for the record books. Unfortunately, all good things have to end. Nevertheless, as we prepared to get ready for our day and Lisa gathered her belongings, the room grew tense. The financial struggles that she discussed the night before were on the top of her mind, with no solution provided. I folded my club clothes from last night and put on a sweatsuit, as I intended to go to the gym. Then it all came together. I wanted to put out an offer that I knew Lisa could not refuse, hoping not to offend her.

07

CHAPTER

ANOTHER ONE

Chapter 7 | Another One

Every Friday typically went the same way. My boys and I meet at a bar and then head over to a strip club. We often did not make it to the strip club because one or all of us would go home with a honey that we met at the bar. Nothing was ever planned. We let the night take us where it wanted us. With a group of four wealthy men, women tend to gravitate towards us. Women probably always come up to us because they see the expensive shit we were drinking or the costly clothes we wore. I never cared what the reason was; it always kept me occupied for the night. Within ten minutes of arriving at the bar, four women who looked almost identical walked up to us. They all had long blond hair and wore a mini skirt with a crop top. I could not tell if they were tall or just the five-inch heels they were wearing. They started talking to us and made it very clear what their intentions were. They giggled at absolutely nothing and pushed their breasts out in our face; they were up to no good. After buying the girls drinks and flirting after a couple of hours of buying the girls drinks and flirting, my friend decided to make the first move. He asked one of the women to go over to his penthouse in the city; the next thing I knew, they were hand in hand walking out of the bar.

What caught me by surprise was when I saw one of my boys whispering in one of their ears. He was married and had a kid.

I was sure his wife was at home taking care of their baby at that moment. They always seemed to have their lives so put-together and even seemed like they were so in love. This perfect image I had about him and his wife all disappeared when I saw his hand too far up the blonde's mini skirt. I would not stop my boy from having a good time, but I would be lying if I said that a part of me did not feel bad for his faithful wife.

Just like that, I was alone at the bar with one of the blonde-haired women.

The three of my friends paired up with a blond and left the bar. Even though they all looked identical initially, I somehow was stuck with the most unattractive blond. Not only that, but she had the personality of a rock. I spent most of the time listening in on my friend's conversation with their blond, but since they were gone, I did not have any other option to try to have a conversation with this one. We both had the same intention of going home together, but she made it impossible to get there. She shoved her ass and boobs in my face, but I was not entertained. I did not even remember her name when I bought her a final drink and left the bar alone.

All my boys were probably having sex with their blond at the same time I was walking alone outside some bar in New York.

I was not ready to go home, so I got in a cab and told him to take me to the best strip club he knew of.

The cab driver did not let me down; we pulled up in front of a bright red building with neon signs all over. I gave him a generous tip before he let me know that I was in Greenwich, Connecticut, and I would need to call for a cab since we were no longer in New York. With that, I walked into the strip club that was blaring loud Spanish music and got myself a drink. It did not take long until I saw a stripper that was dancing for a crowd of people. She looked confident as she did her job, and men were throwing ridiculous amounts of money for her. I think the piles of money around her gave her more confidence as she danced for the men. She had sleek black hair, caramel skin, and piercing brown eyes. She looked like something straight out of a magazine. Her body looked like it had been edited thousands of times, but I was looking at the real thing. Her entire body looked smooth without any imperfections, and she was in ideal shape for her job. I did not take my eyes off her for what felt like hours. Men continued to pay her for her work, but I stood back watching her from afar. If I had to guess, she probably made about a thousand dollars from when I was there. I am sure that I was not the only one that had my undivided attention on her. However, I had a plan. I implemented the plan as soon as she was done dancing and moved off the stage.

I rushed over and offered my hand as she got off the stage. She accepted my hand without acknowledging my presence and continued to walk towards the back of the stage. I gently turned her over to face me and introduced myself with an excellent pick-up line that I do not remember. She seemed impressed and offered a sexy little smile. She was more perfect than when I had seen her on stage. I could not find a single flaw even though I was inches from her face. I gave her a significant amount of money for her fantastic work and offered to buy her drinks after her shift. She accepted the money I handed her and walked backstage without mentioning my offer to drink.

I waited for her without knowing if she would accept my offer. I leaned against a cold wall as I watched other strippers who did not even compare to the one I was waiting for. After about an hour of waiting, the flawless woman walked over to me. This time, she had her hair pulled up in a high ponytail and wore a little black dress that barely covered her tits. She wanted to show off her fantastic body, and I could not blame her. I complimented how she looked, and we left the strip club and walked to the bar across the street. It took me by surprise that she took my hand as we left the club; her confidence showed in every aspect of her.

At the bar, she told me her name was Elena. She had a slight Spanish accent when she spoke, probably because she had moved to Connecticut when she was fifteen from Puerto Rico.

She said intelligently, and I was interested in every word that came out of her lips. Not only was she incredibly sexy, but she also had a brain, unlike the blonde-haired woman from the bar. We talked for a few hours, and I was all about the way she carried herself. She seemed like the whole package. She even offered to pay for the drinks. I thought it was her way of letting me know that she had money and did not need a man to depend on financially. I paid for the drinks, but I would be lying if I said the offer did not turn me on. I called a cab like the previous cab driver suggested driving us back to my place in New York City.

The ride back was long, much longer than I remembered from the passage from the bar to the strip club. Maybe the reason it felt so long was that there was a perfect woman next to me wanting to spend the night with me. We did not talk much on the cab ride to my place. She looked over at me occasionally with those sharp brown eyes, making the sexual tension even more vital. Sometimes, she would wrap her hands around my thigh and slide it up and down while looking at the window. She effortlessly made everything so sexual. Once we got to my apartment, she made herself comfortable as if she lived there.

She slipped her dress off and walked over to me, not lacking any confidence. She walked me over to my room and wasted no time to get what we both wanted.

To my surprise, I woke up to Elena gently rubbing my arm. I was not surprised by how perfect she still looked. It was noon, and I was starving. Usually, I would walk the women I slept without of my apartment the following day. However, I did not want Elena to leave. I asked to take her out for a meal. She not only agreed but also picked a restaurant. Most women could never make up their minds, but you could tell Elena made all the decisions. I liked having a woman who was in charge; it was refreshing for a change.

The restaurant was much fancier than I expected. Not that I cared, I had the money for it. I was just surprised by Elena's choice. We enjoyed our meal, and I was just happy to find an excuse to spend more time with her. After we finished eating, Elena stood up and stated that she already paid for the meal. My mouth flung open, not knowing what to say. The meal must have been over five hundred dollars between the mimosas and the food. I always paid for meals; I felt like it was the least I could do, and I knew I could afford it. She said, "I made enough money last night to cover this meal; let's go."

I was confused; I thought every woman's dream was to have a man pay for everything. We walked out of the restaurant, and I asked her to take her out to dinner next weekend since it was the least I could do.

She gave her infamous small smile, agreed to dinner, and walked away.

A few months passed, and I learned so much more about Elena. Every day we spent time together, I learned something new. I have taken her out on many dates and made sure that I paid each time; the last thing I wanted was to have her pay again. I have never had a more intimate relationship with someone. We fuck a lot, but we also have meaningful conversations. She has opened up to me about her past, and I did the same. I told her about my parents and acted like I did not give a shit about it, but I knew she read me. She and I were not that different. Elena was fiercely independent and lived for other people to see it. She made massive amounts of money stripping but had nothing to show for it. We differed in this aspect. I was good with the money I made and spent it on things that would further my career. People knew that I had money from the shit I wore and the places I went out to eat. I held my reputation because I managed my money well, and Elena had to do the same. One day, we sat down for hours to plan her finances. I taught her how to invest in stocks and property. It did not take long until she could afford her first car; a brand new white Mercedes-Benz. Three months into the relationship and I could not have asked for anything better. I loved that she made a living for herself.

One night I decided to take a drive to Greenwich to visit Elena at work. Stripping was not easy, but she did a great job and made great money doing it. Of course, there was a crowd of men around her when I walked into the strip club. She was dancing and surrounded by piles of cash. She did not see me, but I waited for her towards the back at the end of her performance. She walked right past me without seeing me and walked towards a younger man standing in the corner. He embraced her so that their bodies were touching, and she whispered something in his ear. The next thing I knew, they were both walking out of the club, holding hands and getting into her white Mercedes.

My feelings shifted from being devastated to furious. I did not know which sense I felt more. How could I be so fucking stupid? That is what I deserved for trusting a stripper. I thought things could have been different for us. She was so mature and carried herself like an adult. It turned out she was just a whore like the rest of them. I drove back to the city that night and found another girl to fuck. That will be the last time I'm taken for a fool.

~Six months later~

Six months have passed, and my boys and I did what we did every Friday night. We were drinking beers when I saw Elena from the corner of my eye.

Fucking great, I thought. I ignored her at first, and she continued to laugh loudly while talking to her girlfriend. This was very out of character for her. She was usually pretty chill and did not like to draw attention, but she tried to make herself visible to me. It did not take too much time until she walked up to me. She pulled me away from my friends and apologized for the past six months. She did not bullshit an excuse; instead, she told me everything that happened. She met a guy at the club and, long story short, he was using her for her money.

At first, she thought that their relationship was real and that she could trust him. She paid for everything, and he continued to give her empty promises. During the six months, he drained all her money. She lost her stocks, her money, and her car. Worst of all, she lost her job due to being caught doing drugs at the club. She no longer had an income, and when he saw that, he left her for another girl. She was being used. I wanted to comfort her because I could tell she was hurt, but I did not. She did it to herself. I apologized for what happened to her and walked back to my friends.

I did not know what she wanted me to do. I treated her like a queen when we were together, and I did not do anything wrong. Did she want me to feel sorry and take her back?

One thing was sure; I will never be somebody's second option. After that conversation, I did not see her at the bar that night.

The following day, Elena called me to ask to go out to dinner. I was surprised she kept my number. As much as I wanted to hang up, I agreed to her request. We went to a cheap restaurant, and she did not even offer to pay. Everything we once worked so hard for was down the drain since she decided to be a slut and sleep with another man who was using her for her money. Regardless of it all, we ended up having a good time. At the beginning of the night, I was reserved, but she knew what to say to get me to talk. We laughed like we used to, and she came over to my place after dinner. I noticed that she was not as confident as she once was. She made me make all the first moves. I could tell that she was just as broken as I was. Even though the night with Elena was just like old times, I could not help but feel resentment. After we fucked, she was knocked out on my bed. She probably had too much alcohol because she did not move an inch in hours. I wanted to shake her, wake her up, and yell and all of the shit she put me through. I hardly ever let women stay the night; I did not want to give her the satisfaction of sleeping in my bed. I did not want her to think that she deserved it because we had sex.

I thought of a better idea than waking her up and escorting her to the door. Instead, I stood on my bed like a toddler about to jump up and down, but instead of jumping, I pulled down my boxes and pissed all over Elena. My instincts got the best of me, but I did not care at the time. That was the least she deserved for leaving me for a piece of shit. The alcohol got to my head. After I did my business, I pulled up my boxers and walked to the couch to get some rest. Elena did not move a muscle for the rest of the night, and surprisingly she never brought it up. To this day, I do not know if she never brought it up because she knew she deserved it or if she was too shitfaced even to notice. Whichever it was, I never regretted it because it made me feel better for what she put me through. After deciding to give Elena a second chance, I knew things were going to be different. I was not going to be hurt anymore by a woman. I knew she was more concerned with materialistic things, but she would have to earn these things independently. As much as I enjoy showering my women in gifts, Elena would have to learn to do things alone and without my help. I could have easily hooked Elena up with a stripping gig. I have connections within the city, but I made it her responsibility to find a new job on her own.

I could have driven her to her interviews in Connecticut, but I made her take the train instead.

I am no longer putting myself in the position to be hurt again. If the relationship does not work out again, it would be on my terms, not hers.

08

CHAPHTER

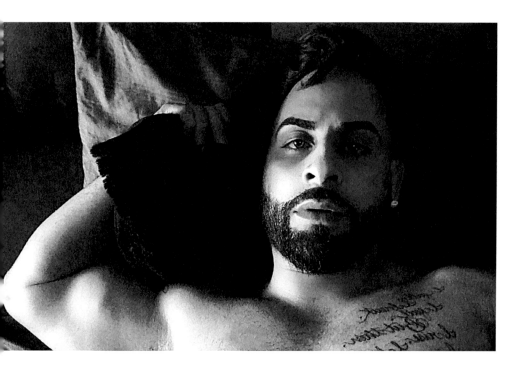

SOME HAVE
NAMES, AND
SOME DON'T

Chapter 8 | Some have Names, and Some Don't

How could I ever forget Leah, this beautiful Jewish girl
from Brooklyn? We met each other through a mutual
friend in a casual phone conversation, and we began to
talk for days and days and days. I could tell right away
that we made a dope connection, but when I saw a picture
of Leah, it was a wrap. She was a gorgeous brown-haired
woman with a tight ass, nice long legs, and the most
beautiful smile that caught my eye. Leah and I fell hard
for each other via telephone while working my ass off, so
it was hard for us to connect for quite some time. I must
admit I thought it was funny that I fell for a girl over the
phone, but Leah just had that way about her. However,
one weekend I had to run to Mystic, Connecticut, for a
weekend seminar. The day I came back, we got together
that evening. It was finally going down, and I must say it
was electrifying. We made "sweet love." I remember that
before I entered her, we looked into each other's eyes, and
she was so moist. I can say this about Leah, not only was
she worth the wait, but the wait made it better.
From that night on, we were together. She did not know
this other shortie named Shayla was my girlfriend, but
she must have wondered how she and I were always
together. Everyone loved Leah. She just had a beautiful
upbeat personality. One day my friend Jose and I
accidentally called her Shayla. Jose has been my friend
for as long as I could remember.

We grew up across the street from each other and have been friends ever since. Leah said, "'What did you just call me?" Jose said, "Leah." She said, "No, you just called me, Shayla!" Jose said, "I slipped and called you Shayla by accident." Leah busted out laughing. I told her we slipped up with the hope of her not getting too upset. I guess it worked because Leah was not bitter at all. That is how cool me and Leah were.

Leah's car was a standard, and to this day, I have never met a female who can handle a stick like her. Girlfriend had skills. We would go to clubs together, she would have her crew, and I would have mine. This was a nice change from the females who never left my side at the club. We would designate a time and a place to meet for our departure, but she and I would find ourselves chilling way before then. Leah did not smoke weed, and that made me happy because I hated that shit.

As my therapy practice began to flourish, I started consulting with other therapists, and on most days, Leah picked me up. Since Shayla lost her job, we hired her as a receptionist, which made things a bit uncomfortable at times. Shayla did not agree to Leah picking me up. It must have embarrassed her, especially in front of all of her work friends. I was oblivious to anyone's feelings except my own. Shayla would say slick comments to Leah, but Leah would not respond.

I long ago asked Shayla to leave Leah alone. I was upfront with Leah about my relationship with Shayla, so she respected it. I could tell she was thirsty to respond to the instigation by Shayla. I must have said to Shayla that Leah and I were just friends, but I am sure Shayla knew otherwise. Leah was just the best girlfriend, as she would do anything for me. I took my cab with my boys one night. It was a snowy winter cold night when we traveled to the Rink in Brooklyn, N.Y. My cab driver dropped us off, and we told him to come back at 2 A.M. That is what time the rink closed. However, it was so crowded that the police shut down Granite Road about two miles before anyone could get to the rink, so the cab could not pick us up. I called Leah at 2 A.M., and by 2:20 A.M., we were all in her car. It was so icy that the car was sliding around the George Washington Bridge. Leah was not even upset, as she was laughing and happy that we called her. Everyone loved Leah because she had the dopest personality.

By this time, Shayla was living in the Bronx with her cousin Precious. They lived on Fulton Ave. It was a big two-bedroom apartment with high ceilings, something that wasn't cheap in that area. This move was the end for Shayla and me. Shayla was working, so she had her own money, which meant she was a lot less dependent on me. Shayla was also maturing and coming into herself.

She now realized her worth and potential. She was a pretty girl, and she saw that she was a diamond with independence and money. In the Bronx, everybody wanted the diamond. She had been so consumed with "Manny" that she never worked on Shayla for the last five years. Now she was doing that. Her cousin Princess and most of her family and friends told her to live life and stop waiting on me. "Manny, he's doing him, so do you?" Slowly these cancerous words spread to her brain. Shayla had been in my ear about going to Six Flags Great Adventures. She knew I was a very spontaneous person. She asked me, "If you and your friends go to Great Adventures, I want to go." I agreed. This was not a problem. I figured she was right. I would probably wake up one day and say, "Today is a nice day for Great Adventures." This is precisely how it happened.

What I am about to tell you is the funniest event in my life, up to this point. The beauty of it is that you can ask Jose if you do not want to take my word on it. This was a hilarious occurrence.

When Leah slept over, we woke up, the sun was shining, and it was a lovely day. I must add that Leah was the only woman I knew whose breath didn't smell bad in the morning. It's like she slept with cinnamon in her mouth. We got out of bed, and I thought, "Today would be a great day for Great Adventures." I ask her while she's showering,

"Do you want to go to Great A?" to which she agreed. I
then called my boy Jose, "Yo, Leah and I are going to
Great A; you with it?" He was down with it. Leah did not
want to be the third wheel with Jose and me, so she
decided to call her cousin in Philly. That was fine with
me. I called Jose back and told him, "Leah's bringing her
cousin for you." "How does she look?" I did not know, so I
asked Leah, who said that her cousin was cute and that
Jose would like her. I relayed the message and waited for
Leah to come out of the shower to call her cousin. Then it
hit me. I had promised Shayla that when I went to Great
A, I would take her. I felt bad. My conscience gets mushy
on me at the weirdest times. I went into the bathroom and
said, "Leah, can Shayla come with us?" She pulled the
shower curtain back and said, "What?" I told her how I
promised Shayla I would bring her to Great A and that if
we were going to go, it would be wrong of me not to invite
her. Leah said, "You're fucking serious?" to which I
responded, "Yeah, I'm serious." "OK, invite her; I got to
see this." All I was thinking was, "Leah is the best; she's
like Jesus Christ's little sister or something."
I called Shayla, and she was in Harlem. "Shayla, you want
to go to Great A with me, Jose and Leah?" "Who?" she said.
"Me, Jose, and Leah." "Jose, you're joking, right?" "No, I
am not joking. I promised you I'd take you when I went,
I'm going, and I want you to come." "OK Jose, when are we
leaving?" I told her, "be ready in about an hour."

I called Jose back and told him the news. Jose said, "What is wrong with you? You can't bring both of them." I said, "Why not? I promised Shayla I would take her, so it is only right to invite her. She wants to go too." Jose said, "The sad thing is that you're dead serious. Manny, if you pull this off, I will bow down to you every time I see you. That will be how I greet you. For the record, I think this is a terrible idea, but I got to see this." I told him to be ready in 30 minutes. Jose had made it like a challenge, like a dare; this was going to be great, I thought. I hopped in the shower, washed up, and Leah and I got dressed to hit the road. Jose stayed with his aunt on Michigan Avenue. We picked him up first. Jose came downstairs just shaking his head as if to say, "Manny, you're crazy." Next, we hit Harlem, and we stopped to get some snacks for our journey. The last stop on this side of the bridge was to pick up Shayla.

We pulled up in front of her building on Bradley Avenue. Shayla was standing on the fire escape; I got out and told her to hurry up and come downstairs. She said, "Manny, you're serious?" I said, "Look, if you're coming, come on; if not, I'm leaving." She said, "I'm coming down now." I got back in the car. Leah was driving, but she often went with her socks instead of wearing shoes. Maybe this was her secret to driving sticks. Jose sat in the back seat. All of a sudden, Shayla came down looking as cute as a button.

She walked to the car and banged the window with her keys. Leah says, "You better tell her something." I rolled down the window. Trina said to me, "You want me to come with y 'all to Great Adventures?" I nodded. She then turned her direction to Leah, "and you're OK with this?" Leah looked up and said, "Look, if you're coming, get in and let's go!" Shayla had to make it awkward when she asked, "Leah, when we start to ride, who is going to be sitting with who?" I said, "I'll sit alone, you two can sit together, or we can rotate every ride." Shayla gave me the weirdest look I have ever seen. She leaned on the passenger side window of the car. Her look said, "Nigga you have lost every ounce of your God damn mind!" Shayla then took out her keys that were tucked in her spandex. She grabbed her pepper spray, reached over me, and started to spray Leah in the face. She said, "I got to go now," and started skipping down Mission Street towards 8th Avenue. Leah jumped out of the car in her socks and chased Shayla down Mission Street.

Meanwhile, Jose and I were lying on the concrete, with tears in our eyes laughing. If you could picture this scene happen, the way Shayla skipped away and Leah chasing her with her socks was hilarious. Jose and I could not stop laughing. Leah missed her, and when she got back to the car, she said, "I'm glad y 'all think it's funny. Get in the car."

We all got in, but we could not stop laughing. Leah kept rubbing her eyes, and that made us laugh even more. She said, "keep laughing, but I'm telling you now, when I see your little girlfriend, I'm going to fuck her up." It was not noon yet, but the day was great. We finally made it to New Jersey. We picked up Leah's cousin, and the four of us went to Great Adventure. We had a blast. Leah and her cousin distracted the staff running the games so that we could win stuffed animal prizes. At the ring toss, Jose and I would jump over the stand, place the ring on the bottle, or complete whatever task the game called for to collect the stuffed animals. We won eight giant stuffed animals and laughed our asses off. Afterward, we went on rides, ate, and even took a nap because I was exhausted. The amusement park had a tram, which you would ride to go from one side to the other. It took you way up high in the air. It took about 10 minutes to get us to the other side. We rode on it, and I was lifted, literally and figuratively. We could not fit all the animals in the car when we were leaving, so we put two in the trunk and one in the back seat with Jose and Leah's cousin. We gave away the others to little kids who did not have a chance at winning any of the games. We went back to the city and ended the day with a smile in the arms of two beautiful women.

A day later, Jose, his girl Natalie, Shayla, and me, went to the movie theater on the east side of Manhattan. I did not have a clue as to what movie we saw. I did know it was a Sunday night. Jose and I were scheming how we were going to ditch our girlfriends once the movie let out. We made many suggestions, like getting a bite to eat and dropping them off, but they were up to our plan. They did not have it tonight. I think it was me who suggested we all go to the Pink Elephant. Once again, Jose gave me the "Manny, are you crazy look." I was just ready for fun, and why shouldn't our ladies have fun too? Shayla and Natalie agreed to go; they would have agreed to anything except letting us out of their sight that evening. When we arrived at Pink Elephant, it was around midnight. We never waited in line or paid to get in, thanks to me being "Fable Manny" and Baby Boy running the spot on Sundays. Inside, it was jumping, as usual. We went to the bar, ordered some drinks, and laid down the deal. "Shayla and Natalie, it's midnight. Let's plan to meet right here at 2:30 A.M." They walked off and left Jose and me at the bar. A half-hour later, Leah came up to me and said, "I told you I was going to fuck her up; remember she started it." Leah then walked off. I did not know what she was talking about; two minutes later, Shayla and Natalie came up to me. Shayla said, "That bitch punched me in the face, go fuck her up!" I said,

"Why didn't you hit her back?" I looked in Natalie's direction and said, "Why didn't you help her out?" Natalie said, "I picked up her earrings." Jose burst out laughing at Natalie's response. Shayla said, "Go fuck her up!" I tried to reason with Shayla. "Shayla, you pepper-sprayed her in the face." I was in love with both of them, what could I do? I could not harm Leah, and I really could not be mad at her because Shayla attacked her first. I said, "Let's go." We left, and I was thinking, "Why didn't she try to fight back?" Shayla talked big shit, and she fucked my ass up every chance she got. I deserved it, and she knew I was not going to hit her back. I did not understand why she did not hit her back as a natural impulse.

One day Leah told me that she was pregnant with my baby. Her eyes beamed with enthusiasm. However, I did not share her enthusiasm. It was not that I did not love her or want to have a child with her. I was more concerned that Shayla would be crushed. I was just young, immature, selfish, and not ready to be with one person. I always assumed that my children would be with Shayla or even one of the many girls I was with. I could not fathom having a child with someone else. My reaction crushed Leah. I was against having a baby and pushed her to have an abortion. At first, she refused, but my attitude probably blew her mind. Leah was more concerned about making me happy.

As a result, she decided to have an abortion. I went with Leah to the appointment at the clinic. After the procedure, she had very little to say to me. This was unofficially our break-up. No one said the words, but I crushed her spirit, making her have an abortion. This was a terrible move on my part. It was one of the first times with a woman that I felt I gave her the wrong advice. I was such an asshole.

To this day, I wish I could take the pain away from Leah. I never regretted her having the abortion, but I knew I was not ready. I was not prepared to be the father of a child who needed me. That was a terrible thing to do, and I wished the whole situation could be reversed. Unfortunately, I have to live with the consequences.

09

CHAPTER

HURT FOR THE
LAST TIME

While they all worked, I visited and played dominoes and popped shit. The supervisor of the back room was this kid Tony. Most of us knew Tony before he moved over to management, so we did not look at him as a supervisor. He did not want beef as long as his workers did their thing to keep the upper management off his back.

When the company moved to a new location, there was only one dude selling cocaine in the company. He often ran out, which I did not understand because his stuff was not always fire. I did not mess with that stuff, but it started to bring the heat on everyone at the job. I taught the guys to cut the bullshit with the drugs and taught them how to make some serious money with gambling and loan sharking. Now they were making steady flow with the cocaine, but nothing like the gambling ring they ran. All I could do was sit back and laugh while watching my boys win.

There was a dress code at the job, but it did not apply to the clerks. They had to look neat and stay fresh. Shayla worked on Mike's floor, but not in his department so that we would see each other daily. Because of this, I played with women when I stopped by work, but not that much. Everyone knew we were an item, but more importantly, they knew Tanya loved Shayla like her own. This made many chicks keep their distance. I still found room to play and work in the city; there was never a shortage of women.

Brandy, the girl I met at Rucker Park, was my lunch date for many days. This is how we got real close. We would have sex on the regular, but our lunch dates were where we bonded.

Even though I was sleeping with Brandy, everyone thought I should be with Shayla. They loved Shayla, so it was a challenging situation. I always listened to everyone's advice but knew what was best for me.

Tanya had no idea I started the gambling ring at work. This was probably embarrassing to her, so I wanted to apologize. I have to tell my story, and this is a part of it. The gambling business was smooth, but she thought it was a terrible idea when Tanya found out. She told the people to tear the business down immediately before being fired, and they complied.

Tanya got a call at the office one day. She answered the phone, and they asked for Vanessa, I think. She was not at her desk, so Tanya asked, "Who is calling?" That way, when she returned, I could let her know. The dude got all crazy like, "Don't worry about who calls." They exchanged words, and Tanya told him the address of the job, like, "bring it, Busta." He said, "I'll be there in 5 minutes." Sonia called me immediately, so I flew over to the office. I grabbed Jose on the way, and we went outside. I am sure glad I got Jose because this man was huge. The dude and I started to beef.

Now I wouldn't say I like to beef, but I had to stick up for
Tanya, especially with Shayla and all the other shorties
looking out the window. He was pissed at me because he
was not backing down. He went to swing at me, but Jose
caught him with a right and then threw him into a parked
car. They were on the car tussling, I punched him
continuously, and I realized I had my fluorescent orange
pocketknife. Just as I reached for it, Tanya stepped in and
broke us up. Thankfully, she stepped in because I was
going to rip homie's face off. The job camera caught
everything, so it is a good thing I did not, or I would have
been in some serious hot water. However, you do that shit
for friends and family. Shayla and I were in our last few
months together. Since she had moved to the Bronx, I saw
a change in her. She was doing her and not me. We went
out one day, and when we returned to her house, I had to
get something from her room. When we entered her room,
her answering machine was blinking. My jealousy took the
best of me, and I told her to play the message. There was
no point in asking because I knew I would do whatever it
took to hear the news. She was not moving fast enough, so
I pressed play. She then ran to the machine, pulled out
the cassette, and began to unravel the tape. I got pissed
and left.

She clearly showed that she was hiding something. She
looked as guilty as she ran to the answering machine.

It is somewhat silly that I would get pissed since I am with so many women, but I did not like it in return.

Shayla was constantly slapping roughhousing or me, but I would usually defend myself. I started to get irritated because Shayla was possessive. If my boys were waiting for me to go to a club, Shayla would take my keys and sit in front of the door to prevent me from going. I would try to move her out of the way. We would be laughing because it was funny, but it began to get ridiculous. Me trying to drag her, and she is holding the doorknob for dear life. I would unlock the top lock, and she would lock the bottom, then I would open the bottom, and she would close the top. In these instances, she would sometimes bite me, not hard, but enough to let me know she did not like it when I went out without her. I liked the craziness at first because it showed that she wanted me, but it was starting to get out of control.

A man should never hit a woman. In a relationship, once you start hitting, be it a man or woman doing the hitting, it is time to go. Rarely does it get better? If I get to the point of hitting a female, then there is no respect. No respect means we should not be together.

Shayla and I made up, but a few weeks later, she went away. I called her house and cracked her answering machine code.

How I did it; persistence. When the messages played, I did not like what I heard. There were two messages from the same person, and they were not messaging a girl with a boyfriend. When I asked her, she brushed it off as me bugging out and overreacting. When a partner in a relationship is sneaky, it is never a good sign.

Shayla was giving me a taste of my own medicine, and I was going loco. I could not take it. I was not too fond of the way it felt. I told myself, "fuck her,"
but I now realized I loved her. I could not just let go. It was a terrible place to be in and extremely dangerous. I was ready to kill.

It got so crazy; my left arm swelled up on me. It was like a balloon, and it felt as if it would pop if you touched it. I went to the hospital, and the doctors admitted me. They had all types of specialists come to look at my arm. They took all kinds of tests, but the experts did not know what was wrong with my arm. I knew. It was "jealousy." They did surgery to drain fluid and kept me for a couple of days. I had a few visits and got to know the hospital quite well. My shorty Brandy would come through, and we would get it on. She would do whatever it took to make a man happy. We did some things that should never be done in a hospital. It was not a surprise that she later went into the pornography industry.

When I was released, my boy Jose from the Polo Grounds picked me up and went to the movie theater to see "Untouchables." I was a bit dizzy since I continued to take the pain meds the doctor prescribed. As the film progressed, the screen kept flashing, and I was getting dizzy and felt woozy. Then I just threw up. Jose said, "Let's go, man." We left, and I told him to drop me at Shayla's. When Jose dropped me off, the light in her room was on. I told him goodbye, and he left. I then rang Shayla's intercom, but no one answered. I went outside to call her to the window, but now Shayla's room light was off. I am thinking, "These meds are strong as fuck cause I know the light was just on." I wanted to call her, so I walked to the corner payphone on Richards Avenue. The phone rang and Shayla's cousin, Precious, answered. She told me Shayla was not home, but I knew I heard Shayla's voice when she first responded.

I was getting tight cause these fucking broads are trying to play me. It is like 9 P.M., and the block is empty. I went in front of the building and tried to reach the fire escape; I had to jump to get it. My injured arm would not allow me to jump. By the graces of God, I saw a metal garbage can. I turned it upside down and got on it. I climbed up on the fire escape and made it to Shayla's window. I climbed in. All the lights were off, so I walked out of her room into her cousin's room. I hit the light switch, and there are Shayla, Precious, and a guy named Tiny.

They were stuck and busted, and I felt like a fucking crazed stalker. I called Shayla and her cousin every type of bad name in the world. I turned to leave, and Shayla was calling me. When I got to the door, I cursed her out some more and left. Shayla let me go, as this was an indication she was sleeping with a homeboy. The old Shayla from the Bronx would never have let me leave being that mad at her. This new Bronx creature was the devil.

I was extra mad because weeks prior, I was with Shayla and her cousin, introducing me to Tiny. I felt like, how could you introduce me to the guy you are fucking? Thinking back to that moment, I felt like a fucking idiot for being the only one between the four of us, not knowing what was going on. This was the reason for my trust issues. My pride was hurt. I had never been hurt like that ever, and I vowed never to let a female get that much control of me. This was entirely no good in my eyes. No one should be able to get you off your square like that. I hated Precious for polluting my innocent Shayla.

Shayla swore up and down she was only braiding Tiny's hair, and like a fool in love, I came back. The final straw came like two weeks later. The last red flag came when I was with Jose, and we went to Shayla's. She was coming downstairs as we were ringing her intercom. She said, "Come with me to the store." As we were walking to the store, a van kept circling the block crazy slow.

We were crossing the street on an angle on our way back from the store, and the van was cruising behind us. I said to Shayla, "who the fuck is that?" She said, "That's my cousin." Now I have been sleeping with this girl forever, and I know this dude is no cousin. I walked to the van, and I am like, "Who are you?" He said, "Tommy." Then he says to Shayla, "I thought you ain't with him no more?" I said, "Word, Shayla, you don't mess with me no more; you could have told me." She said, "I didn't say that, Manny." I said, "It doesn't even matter, take me upstairs so I can get all of my clothes. I'm done with you." I went upstairs, got my stuff, and Jose and I walked uptown to the Bronx. I said, "That's it for her, my name is Manny, and I ain't nobody's bitch." A few weeks later, Shayla got in a bad car accident and was hospitalized for a week. Jose went to visit her, and Shayla was asking where I was. I never went. My pride was crushed. I slept with hundreds of girls, and they know I would wig out if they touched Shayla. I never put her in harm's way.

My feelings about my decision not to visit Shayla went back and forth. I knew I was wrong for not going to see her. I was sorry for that, but I would not have done anything differently. She was the only woman who ever hurt me, and I vowed never to let that ever happen again.

10

CHAPTER

SOMETHING TO
LISTEN TO

I thought I never wanted to see Kayla again after she embarrassed me by talking to the guy at the bar. He was some cheap asshole who just wanted to take her home that night. I invested time in her, our relationship, and her career. She was selfish and not thinking about all the possibilities that she received from our relationship. If she truly understood what I had to offer her, she would have never chosen another man over me.

I did not talk to Kayla for months, and I did not feel the need to. She was the one who was benefiting from the relationship, not me. It was not until I ran into Kayla at the same bar that I punched that dick flirting with her. She was sitting alone this time. I saw her curls from across the bar, and the next thing I knew, I was ordering two expensive drinks for both of us. This may have been my way of showing off, but I did not care. She looked shocked when she heard me ordering the drinks. I grabbed both glasses and handed her one. She somehow looked even more amazed, thinking I bought the drink for someone else. There was still anger built up inside of me, but I did not let her see it. Instead, we caught up on everything that we have missed over the past few months. We continued to drink for the night, and she came home with me.

I woke up earlier than Kayla did the following day. I took a shower, and when I walked into my room, she had just woken up. I saw the panic in her eyes when she looked at the time and realized that it was almost noon. After swearing for about two minutes, I asked her what was wrong. She explained that it was her niece's first birthday and her sister was having a huge birthday party in the city. She put her hair up into a high ponytail with a few loose curls falling out of the ponytail. When I realized that I was not as attracted to Kayla as I once was, she was pretty, but I was not as captivated by her. As she was reapplying for her makeup, she asked me if I wanted to go to a birthday party for her baby niece with her. I quickly denied; why the fuck would I want to spend my Saturday at a baby's birthday party? Kayla asked again, this time looking me in my eyes. With hesitation, I agreed. I figured that I should put in an effort if Kayla and I would fix our relationship. I did not think she deserved my time, but I did not have anything planned for the rest of the day anyways.

After Kayla finally settled on a shade of lipstick, we left for the party. She had no option but to wear the same dress she wore last night, which was inappropriate for a one-year-old's birthday party.

It was a forty-minute drive, and I regretted going to this stupid party every second of the ride.

I didn't even know Kayla had a niece, and she barely spoke about her sister. There were about a hundred people drinking champagne next to a cake that looked like a wedding cake when we arrived. A server handed us each a glass when someone approached us. It was Kayla's sister holding a baby, whom I assumed was Kayla's niece. I pretended to be interested in the conversation when I spotted a fine woman across the room. Her milky skin complimented her hazel eyes perfectly. Shit, she was probably the hottest female I have ever seen in New York. I suddenly started not regretting coming to the party. As Kayla and her sister carried a conversation about something that I was uninterested in, I made eye contact with the hot woman across the room. I created distance between Kayla and myself so that she knew that I was available. She smiled slightly and then looked away. Kayla kept complaining that she did not feel well and that she was too hungover. After she decided to go to the bathroom, the hot girl I saw earlier walked up. That was the most nervous I have ever been to talk to anyone. She introduced herself, "Hey, my name is Maya. I saw you walk in with my cousin. She talks about you all the time; it's a pleasure to meet you finally." Fuck, of course, they had to be related.

A part of me was hoping that they did not know each other to have a chance with Maya.

I introduced myself, and we shook hands. The interaction went much more professionally than I wanted it to. Kayla was taking a long time in the bathroom, but I did not care if that meant that I have to spend more time with her cousin. She made subtle remarks about Kayla saying, "She was not much fun" and "not the best actress." I ignored the comments about Kayla but could not forget when she mentioned that she was a model, which did not surprise me. Her body and her looks should be posted everywhere for the world to see. She explained how she started modeling her feet and hands for commercials, but her absolute dream was to become an actor. She abruptly walked away, which initially left me confused. Then I realized Kayla was behind me. Why did Maya look guilty when she saw Kayla? She must want something more than a friendship with me, or else she would not have reacted the way she did. Kayla looked awful, and it was visible that she was pale and weak. She said that she was sick and had to leave immediately. I was upset that my chances of getting to know Maya was ruined because Kayla could not handle her liquor.

When I got home after dropping Kayla off, I took off my jean jacket and realized that something was in the pocket. I pulled out a piece of paper with ten digits written on it and a note that said, "I'm much more fun than her."

I knew that it was Maya's since she was the only one close enough to slip it into my pocket. I felt my heart beat faster when I realized that Maya was interested in me, the same way I was interested in her. She did not care that I was seeing her cousin, and I did not either. Maybe I would have felt a little guilt if Kayla did not let every guy feel her up. Nevertheless, I just wanted to get to know Maya. I loved the way that her bold and beautiful appearance matched her personality. I waited four days until I texted Maya; I did not want to seem too desperate. She responded a few hours later and agreed to dinner. I felt like a child going on their first date. Maya was beautiful and was unique compared to any girl that I have ever been with. I picked out a clean white tee and a fresh pair of pants that have never been worn. I had to look my best to keep up with her. I drove to the Italian restaurant, and Maya was already there; she looked at a menu but still managed to look like a supermodel. I had always liked when women showed up earlier than I to date did. It shows that they have nothing to prove and do not care about being "fashionably late." She was wearing a tight silver dress that showed off her body perfectly. Her hair was straightened, and not a single hair was out of place. I thought she could not have looked better than how she did at the party, but I was wrong. She would be the only person I would forgive for using the excuse of being fashionably late because she looked perfect.

We sat at the restaurant for hours. We ordered drinks and continued our conversation that we started at the party. I remembered her telling me about wanting to be an actor, so I surprised her with an interview for a television show. When I told her the news, she giggled like a young girl. She told me that I would not regret it because she was a much better actor than Kayla was. Before I had time to respond, she stood up from the table and gave me a long intimate kiss in the middle of the restaurant. I was hoping that everyone was looking; I wanted to show that girl off to the world. It took me by surprise, but I was happy that she accepted my offer. I would not have offered her this opportunity if I did not think that she could do it. She was beautiful, well-spoken, intelligent, and funny. She was meant to be a star.

Maya called me thrilled after her audition; the producers gave her the part on the spot. I was not surprised. This was the stepping-stone for her acting career. Maya thanked me over ten times on the phone and was very grateful for the opportunity that I gave her. She asked to see me that night to thank me for the audition personally. There was only one issue; I already had plans with her cousin, Kayla. I lied, of course, and told her I had to work, but I wanted to blow Kayla off to see Maya.

Not only was Maya hotter, but she was more appreciative of our relationship. I would rather spend time with Maya any day of the week than Kayla, but I knew I could not blow Kayla off again.

Kayla came over, and it felt like torture knowing that I could've been with Maya instead. There was something about Kayla that didn't let me let her go. She noticed that something was wrong, and she asked why I had been acting weird. I told her that I was working like a dog, lying, of course. She kept asking me questions, and I continued to lie. I knew if I told her the truth, she would leave, and I did not want that. She looked upset before asking me, "You've been acting real shady lately. Are you seeing other bitches? If you are, I'm out. I know I made that mistake, but I promised never to do that again". I did not know how to respond. Worst of all, I did not believe her. For all I knew, she was talking to other guys and was using me for money. I was unsure if I was hesitant to believe her because of how she made me feel or because I wanted to justify my relationship with her cousin. I avoided her question and ended the night off with a lie. I told her that I was sick and needed to be alone. She seemed hesitant to leave, but the cab I bought her was outside. The second she left, I called Maya immediately to come over.

Maya and I had a blast. Our relationship was business-related, but we still managed to have fun. The night she came over, we wrote scripts together and still had a good time. After working for the night, Maya put the scripts away and jumped on me. In between every kiss, she was thanking me, and she seemed so grateful. Kayla would have never done this for me. We spent the rest of the night having sex and feeling appreciated for each other's company.

It did not take long for people to start recognizing Maya on the street. Her role on the television was a hit, and she was terrific at it. She worked hard, and it showed. She even received a call from a producer to audition for a movie lead. She was so excited and did not show an ounce of fear to be auditioning for a lead. She asked me to be her date to the movie premier if she got the part. I agreed, trying not to show my hesitation. She must have noticed my delay in words when she said, "Don't worry, Kayla will have no right to be mad. We both know that she could have never made it as far as me". However, I was worried about Kayla, who was already skeptical. Not only that but all the other women who I also see. Maya was on the road to being famous, and if pictures were taken and posted in a magazine, I knew it would be game over for all my other relationships. They would all know that Maya's fame would have had something to do with me.

All I did for Kayla was buy her an acting agent when I offered Maya an audition for a show that launched her career. I made myself feel better by telling myself that we would not have been in this position if Kayla were not such a whore. It gave me a sense of comfort at the moment to feel like I was doing the right thing.

To no one does surprise, Maya has the lead for the movie. It was only a couple of weeks after until it was the night of the movie premiere. I have done many things in my life but never go to a movie premiere, especially when I was dating the main character. I put on my expensive black-on-black suit to walk Maya down the aisle of the red carpet. Maya looked stunning in her sparkly gold dress and four-inch heels. Everyone was taking pictures of Maya as she walked like a supermodel down the red carpet. At that moment, no one knew who I was, and they did not care. All the attention was on the gorgeous female who had her hand in mine. She was meant to be a movie star.

11

CHAPTER

PULL MY
JACKET:
AMY'S POV

Chapter 11 | Pull My Jacket
Amy's POV

I will never forget when I first saw Manuel. It was our first day of middle school. He was wearing a colorful jacket and light baggy jeans. He looked nervous, so I walked up to him and introduced myself, "Hi, my name is Amy. It's my first day of middle school too." I must have looked ridiculous, with my blue overalls and two pigtails that my big sister did for me before school. I had no fears when I was younger, and I did not care what others thought of me. I would have never repeated this action in my adulthood. However, I do not think Manuel cared what I was wearing. We instantly clicked. We had all of our classes together and never left each other's side. We bonded over many things, the main thing being hip-hop. We spent hours after school just listening to music and not speaking a word.

Our friendship grew stronger over the next couple of years. We shared all our secrets, even the deepest ones that we never told anyone else. We both grew up without our parents and were raised by our grandmothers. I was lucky enough to have an older sister; Manuel was an only child. I always felt bad because he never had friends at home, so I promised him that I would always be his best friend. I always knew that our friendship was unique, and I cared for him more than anyone else in the entire world.

Our friendship continued to grow until one day, Manuel told me that he had a secret that he has never shared with me. Frightened by what he might say, I stayed silent. He broke the silence when he said, "My biggest secret is that I like you, Amy. I promised that I would never lie to you." The next thing I knew, my lips were attached to his, and we were sharing our first kiss in the lunchroom of our middle school. We were instantly surrounded by childish remarks around us, which continued until a teacher separated us. Although the kiss only lasted about four seconds, it was the most magical thing that has ever happened to me.

In high school, we were known as the couple who have been inseparable since the first day of middle school. Our friendship blossomed into a relationship where Manuel became my first boyfriend. We spent every day together listening to music, taking walks at the park, and occasionally skipping school to spend alone time together. My favorite memories were the ones we spent talking about our future. We planned on going to college, getting well-paid jobs, and traveling the world. We wanted to experience the world together. Most importantly, we planned to have a handful of kids where we could raise them, unlike our parents.

Manuel and I hardly ever got into any fights. At the time, I thought that people who loved each other as much as we did never had to fight. We were perfect together, and nothing was ever going to get in the way of us. On the other hand, so I thought.

It was not until the end of our senior year of high school that Manuel crushed my heart and told me that he could not commit to a relationship after high school. He told me that he wanted to explore the world and experience all the things he has been restricted to throughout the years. We were supposed to do those things together, I thought. All the promises that he told me were lies, and I was angry. How could he change his mind after all those years of planning our future? I could not have been the only one who was fooled; we were even voted the cutest couple for the yearbook! He was the only reason I applied to college. The school was not for me, but we had a plan of maintaining a long-distance relationship throughout college. After constantly begging Manuel to take me back for a couple of weeks, I decided to wait no longer and enlisted in the Army. Our graduation was in a couple of weeks, and I could no longer let Manuel control my future. Manuel and I did not speak after high school. We went from best friends to lovers, to strangers. I did not throw any of his letters, gifts, or pictures away. Even though I was only eighteen at the time, I knew that our love was pure and meant to last a lifetime. There was not much space to pack to basic training, but I made room for a small Polaroid picture of Manuel and me. We looked so in love. We were dressed in the freshest 90s clothing; I was wearing a white tee tucked into a plaid skirt while Manuel wore a striped button-down and jeans.

It was not until the end of our senior year of high I was kissing him on the cheek while he smiled at the camera showing all of his teeth. I tucked that picture between my underwear and shirts, making sure that nothing would happen to it. The next day was my first day at Fort Dix. The first day of my future did not include the love of my life.

I hated my first few months in the Army, although it probably was better than college. I believed that part of the reason I hated it so much was because this was never part of my plan. If I had time to adjust to the idea of being part of the military, I think I would have liked it more. I met a few good people, even a man who showed interest in me. He was a couple of years older, and I referred to him as Moore, as many people in the military call each other by their last names even if they are friends. We did not have too much downtime in basic training, but he made himself present whenever possible. I was not interested in getting to know anyone else on a personal level, not after Manuel. However, spending time with Moore was an excellent outlet to get my mind off things, and he was good company.

We were hardly ever allowed to make phone calls, and there was not much time to write letters to our loved ones. I took any opportunity to write letters. I wrote letter after letter to someone who did not want anything to do with me.

Deciding that I could not waste my life on Manuel, I decided to give a chance to Moore. He was kind, but he was not my childhood sweetheart. He had bright blue eyes; he was strong and had the muscles to prove it. He grew up in an affluent household with both his parents in Texas. He made it clear that he was excited when I started to reciprocate feelings towards him. We made the best out of the rest of our time at basic training. We ate lunch next to each other, even though we were not allowed to look at each other. We had to eat, sitting straight and looking forward. I felt like a robot during most of my time at Fort Dix, except for my time with Moore. We did not have much time to sleep; however, we spent much of that time talking and getting to know each other on a more personal level. It was not until a few weeks before basic training ended that he kissed me and told me that he loved me. The kiss could not have even compared to the kiss I had in my middle school lunchroom, but I told him that I loved him back.

Instead of going back home after basic, Alex Moore, whom I referred to as his first time by this point, decided to travel to Texas to meet his family. He asked me to be his girlfriend three months before our trip to Texas. I would be lying if I did not compare every aspect of our relationship to my prior one.

His family was very welcoming when we visited. It was everything that I wished for as a child; two loving parents, a brother, and a sister who were close in age. Alex was fortunate. His parents threw a huge family barbeque as a congratulatory gift to Alex and me. I thought it was extreme, but Alex seemed excited. At the dinner table, Alex stood up to make an announcement. His siblings and parents looked up at him as if he was a celebrity at that moment. His mother, who was sitting next to me, started to get teary eyes. I thought it was a bit odd, but I figured that was just the family's dynamic. The next thing I knew, Alex was down on one knee and asking me to marry him. Without knowing how to respond, I offered a small smile and looked around at his family, wondering if it was some prank. His mother had her hands over her mouth, and his little sister was filming on her iPhone. Trying to get the image of Manuel out of my head, I shook my head in a "yes" motion and kissed him. His entire family began to clap, and Alex held my arm in the air as if he was claiming victory. The rest of the visit in Texas consisted of questions regarding the wedding. With each question came nausea. I was not ready for any of it. I felt like I just met Alex, and he proposed out of nowhere. I learned his dad was in the Army when he was our age.

He met Alex's mom right when he came home from basic training, and he proposed to her four months after. After being told this story, I knew where Alex's inspiration came from. He wanted to be married before one of us was inevitably deployed, but nothing about this situation made sense to me.

My flight home to Connecticut was a long one. A few of my friends picked me up from the airport. They made "welcome home" signs and were all waiting with smiles on their faces. It took only a few minutes for one of my friends to notice the new ring on my finger. Suddenly, I was being bombarded with questions in the middle of the airport. My mind jumped from how I would tell my sister and grandma about suddenly having a fiancé, all the shit I was put through in basic training, but most importantly, seeing Manuel. I agreed to answer all their questions over dinner.

I described how I met Alex, how he showed interest in me first, and how he proposed a couple of weeks prior in Texas. "Those military men certainly do not waste any time," my friend Jen said. She was not wrong; I did not expect an engagement to happen in less than a year of knowing Alex. We never even spoke about our future. "I'm not going to lie to you, Ames; I honestly thought Manuel flew to New Jersey and proposed when I saw the ring," Jen continued.

I wished it were true; I wish he wrote me back and was the one I would be married to. Pretending, as I didn't care, I asked, "What's that sorry mother fucker up to now anyway?" They explained that he no longer goes by Manuel but Fable Manny. He was doing well for himself and was doing all the things he planned to do in high school, just without me. Knowing that he was doing so well for himself made me slightly aggravated, even though I should have been happy for him.

Settling back at home was a bit of a struggle. My grandma and sister supported my engagement, but I am sure they knew I was still stuck on "Fable Manny." To get my mind off things, I decided to take a run. I found myself running faster than I ever have. I was filled with frustration and fear, and I felt like my feet could not keep up with my mind. I was at the park that Fable Manny and I used to go to the next thing I knew. We used to lay down under the tree in the middle of the park and talk about our future. Besides a man walking on his own, who I thought was Fable Manny at first glance, the park was empty. After reminiscing on memories that now mean nothing, I ran back home in a full sprint.

That night, I got dressed in my best attire. One of the good things that came out of basic training was losing a few pounds in all the right places. My waist was more petite, making my ass seem even more prominent. I wore the tightest black dress I could find and a pair of silver heels.

I wore my hair down for the first time in months, and I felt like a new woman. Walking into the restaurant with my friends, I saw someone that looked like Fable Manny again. Except for this time, it was him. I walked up to him, and before I knew it, my hand was making a swinging motion towards his face. I slapped him so hard he barely had time to react. Before he had the chance to say anything, my friends grabbed me by my wrists and walked me out of the bar.

I felt awful. How could I react so childishly? Isn't going into the Army supposed to make you more mature or some shit? I did not know what to do. I didn't know what I was going to tell Alex. There is no way to rationalize slapping your ex-boyfriend. Jen saw the panic in my eyes and offered to help. She told me she had Fable Manny's number and that she would give it to me under one condition if I apologized for assaulting him. She knew that he meant a lot to me and did not want our relationship to be ruined by my sudden act of violence.

The following night I hesitated to call Fable Manny. Would he be too angry to talk to me? The next thing I knew, the phone was ringing. "Yo, what's up?" He didn't think it was me on the other end of the line. "Hey, it's Amy. I'm sorry for yesterday. I was frustrated and--" next thing I knew, I was interrupted by a deep voice. "I was a dick for not responding to your letters, don't worry about it.

Just don't let it happen again. Yo, I didn't even know you were back from basic training." The next thing I knew, we were on the phone for hours. We talked about everything under the sun, except for Alex and my engagement. I felt a wave of guilt hover over me when we hung up the phone. How could I be such a horrible fiancé to Alex? I would have to tell Fable Manny over dinner we planned the following night.

We decided to hang out as friends. After all, we were friends before we ever got into a relationship. Without making it seem like I was trying too hard, I put a light layer of makeup on and put my hair in a half ponytail. I slid into my tightest jeans and decided on a loose red blouse. I never thought I would be seeing Manuel, I mean, Fable Manny again. He was already at the restaurant when I arrived; he stood up and greeted me with a kiss on my cheek. I instantly felt feelings that I never felt with Alex. I sat down and immediately told him about Alex, knowing that I could not have hidden my engagement ring for long. He looked happy, genuinely happy for me. I wished I were as comfortable as he thought I was. He even asked if he would be invited to the wedding, which was a question I chose to ignore. The last thing I would want is to have a wedding where I would marry someone in the crowd rather than the groom. We continued our dinner as friends as Alex was the last thing on my mind, and I was falling in love with my best friend all over again.

The next few days at home felt like an eternity. I kept seeing Fable Manny everywhere I went, except it was not him, just my imagination. I knew that I had to tell Alex. I knew I had to tell the man who loved me that I was in love with someone else. His family was going to be devastated. Without much thought, I called Alex; he picked up the phone and said, "Hey honey, I haven't talked to you in a while! How have you been? I miss you." My end of the line was filled with sobs. I told him everything. We cried on the phone together before we decided what was best for us. We decided to end things. Four years have passed, and my time in the Army was ending. Four years that I would never wish to repeat. I did not re-enlist, but Alex did. Alex and I remained friends throughout our time in the military. I decided not to get into any relationships until I knew I was ready. I never seemed to be prepared because my heart still belonged to one person. When I got home, I knew exactly whom I wanted to see. This time, I never had to worry about being deployed or being away from home. I called Fable Manny, and we made plans.

I walked into his apartment and courageously stepped up to him and kissed him. Without hesitation, he kissed me back. I told him that Alex and I ended things, but I do not think he cared. He must have always known that I never stopped loving him, and I hoped that he never stopped loving me.

He congratulated me for my time in the service and continued to kiss me. The next thing I knew, we were in his bed. It was as if we never skipped a beat.

12

CHAPTER

GHOST HOUSE: FABLE MANNY'S POV

Chapter 12 | Ghost House
Fable Manny's POV

I knew my ass was out of shape when I went on a run and could only run half a mile. I used to run several miles without a problem. I was fast, too; I would pass every runner at the park. No one was able to keep up with me. I was not fat by any means, but I was not as slim as I once was. I was once comfortable running without a shirt on, but I would not even think about doing that now. I also lost some muscle definition, which I was told was hot from many females. Not wanting to lose to my physique that attracted women, I decided to get back into the gym. Finding time for the gym was difficult with my busy lifestyle. Not many people hustle as hard as I do and juggle so many women. I thought of going to the gym as an investment for all my relationships. For my first day back at the gym, I decided to wear black basketball shorts, a grey short sleeve shirt, and a brand new pair of Adidas. I walked into the gym confidently, not wanting anyone to notice and label me as "the new guy." I acted as if I had been to this gym a million times and that I knew where everything was. I took a seat on the first bench that I saw open, avoiding the treadmills and elliptical because that would have been a clear indicator that I did not know what I was doing.

I decided to start with a chest press, which I have not done in over a year. Still not wanting anyone to notice that I have not lifted in so long, I loaded the barbell with forty-five-pound plates, totaling one hundred thirty-five pounds.

I laid flat on the bench and raised the barbell above my chest, and the next thing I knew, my arms could not support the weight. The barbell came crashing down towards my chest. The weight that was once easy to lift was now crushing my chest. I did not want anyone to notice the man who could not lift one hundred thirty-five pounds, so I laid quietly with the barbell on my chest for a few seconds. Before knowing my next move, I saw small pale hands that lifted the bar from my body. Still in a panic, I sat up and laid eyes on the most beautiful woman I had ever seen. She had perfect features, long blond hair, big blue eyes, nice plump lips, and the fittest body that I have ever seen. She was wearing leggings with a sports bra, and it showed off her body perfectly. "You've got to be careful there, big guy. Don't be afraid to start with low weight." I still didn't know how to respond; I was embarrassed that I was helped by a female that probably weighed half of what I do. "I'm Manuel, but everyone calls me Fable Manny," I said without knowing what else to say. She let out the sexiest laugh, tilted her head back, and introduced herself as Ashley. When she asked if I was new to the gym, I lied and said that I have been coming here for years. I think Ashley caught my lie.

The gym went much better than I was expecting. Besides almost dying from my first five minutes at the gym, I met the sexiest woman. Ashley offered to assist me for the rest of my workout, which was easiest to agree to. She made sure to go easy on me, even though she did not admit it; she knew I was getting back into the gym. Occasionally, she would get inappropriately close to show me a new workout. I pretended my heavy breathing was from lifting the weights, but it was all due to the female rubbing up against me at the gym. I almost felt stupid for not asking her out, but a female like her must already be taken. I rearranged my priorities to go to the gym every day simultaneously in hopes of seeing Ashley. The rest of my day was spent trying not to think about the sexy blonde-woman person from the gym. My muscles were sore, but I knew one thing was sure. I was going to the gym to see Ashley tomorrow.

I woke up much earlier than I wanted to. I brushed my teeth and put on my most expensive workout clothes. I rushed to the gym, and the beautiful blond was the first thing I noticed when I walked in. I was no longer worried about everyone seeing me; I was concerned about others noticing Ashley. My jealousy had already begun for the girl whom I only met once. She somehow looked hotter than yesterday in a hot pink crop top with white leggings.

She was doing a crazy workout that required her to go from pull-ups to mountain climbers without rest. After she finished her set, I walked up to her. I told her that she was "killing it," and she smiled. She gave me a few recommendations for my workout, and I left her to finish hers. During my entire training, I kept Ashley in view. I think she was used to being looked at because she never once turned her head to look for me. I had the best workout using Ashley's recommendations and watching her workout.

I had to take the next two days off from the gym. I was so sore I felt like I could not move a muscle without grunting. I spent my recovery time with the gym-seeing women. There were moments when I was with them and thought of Ashley. None of them even compared to her. What was even better was that she has the most charming personality. She was kind to everyone and always offered to help. This was evident at the gym; I have witnessed her providing help to older women who need it. She was an angel who seemed to care about other people more than she did. Ashley was not my usual "type," but it is hard not to like perfection. I was looking forward to my time back at the gym.

The following day I grew with excitement, knowing I would see Ashley at the gym. As I was walking into the gym, Ashley was walking out. Shit, she was leaving. "Hey, Fable Manny, I missed you the past couple of days! Were my workouts too tough for ya?" she joked.

Pretending that I wasn't still sore from her workout, I lied and told her that I was busy with work. She nodded, pretending to know the lifestyle that I lived. We chatted for a few minutes before she asked me if I had a girlfriend. Technically, I had a handful.

Nevertheless, she did not need to know that. I was shocked by her question and nodded my head no. For the first time, I was asked on a date. The feeling of a female taking charge was sexy to me, and I agreed to the date for a million reasons.

I was attracted to Ashley more than anyone was. She liked me without knowing how much money I had, without offering her career opportunities, knowing that I was not as strong as I used to be, and she helped me without wanting anything in return. For that reason, I wanted to make our first date special. I decided to plan it all since Ashley was the one who asked me out. I did something that I never did before. I cooked dinner, the most expensive steak at the store, and russet potatoes. I wanted to cook something moderately healthy since Ashley looks like she eats nothing but salad. Ladies usually cooked for me, but I was willing to do anything to make Ashley mine. Ashley looked like she jumped off the cover of a magazine and into my living room. She wore a long pencil skirt with a white lace tank top. It was like a real-life Barbie was standing in front of me. Her long eyelashes and red lipstick mesmerized me; I was not used to seeing her with makeup since we only talked at the gym.

We ate dinner together, and she complimented my cooking with every bite she took. I do not know if she was honest, but I felt accomplished. After we ate, we headed to the couch to watch T.V. We shared many of the same interests and watched many of the same shows.

We decided to watch a new documentary about extraterrestrial beings. We watched about half a season before she was asleep on my shoulder. I let her sleep as I paused the documentary since I promised her that I would not watch it without her. When I reached for my phone, I had several unread texts. I knew they were from other girls that I have been dating. I instantly felt bad for Ashley. I usually did not feel guilty for talking to several girls at once, but Ashley was pure and liked me for who I was, not for what I could offer her.

She woke up an hour later and still managed to look perfect. "Good morning," I said jokingly. Without responding, she wrapped her legs around my waist and kissed me. I picked her up and brought her to the bedroom. I gently dropped her on my bed and did what I did best. I woke up the next morning feeling the best that I have ever felt. I had the most passionate sex with the most incredible woman. I walked her out and agreed to see her again, preferably not at the gym.

Ashley and I have had many dates since. We have been together for a year, and she has never failed to amaze me. She was the most serious relationship amongst all of the others. She cared for me and expected nothing in return. She has kept me interested in the gym, kept me company during horror documentaries, and has kept me entertained by having sex. She was the closest I have come to romantically loving a woman, fuck; I may even have loved her. There was no way in hell that I would have let her know that.

I was struggling with an internal conflict. I felt like I could potentially have a future with Ashley, but not if I was sleeping around with all other women. I liked the other women I slept with, but not like Ashley. There were several times when I blew them off to hang out with Ashley. Not only was she the best lover, but she was also a best friend. I knew that she was the best option to raise a family with. She was everything that would make up a perfect mother, loving, caring, and genuine. Getting older never gets easier, and it requires people to make decisions and quickly. Feeling a wave of guilt, I did the unthinkable. I bought Ashley and me a gym.

I knew buying a gym would be an excellent investment for our careers. It was always an excuse to spend more time with Ashley while working.

She was taken aback when I first told her about the news. She was the only girl who was unaware of all the money I had, and I wanted to keep it that way. I lied and told her that I had a perfect credit score, making it extremely easy to buy the gym. Ashley trusted me more than she trusted any person I have ever met. She believed everything I told her and never questioned me. She never called me to "check up on me." I knew she was not suspicious of my whereabouts. She knew I was a hard worker and worked all hours of the day. Knowing that Ashley trusted me so much made it that much harder to lie to her.

We agreed to be physical trainers. Now that I was fit enough to train others, I trained the men, and Ashley would train the women. Ashley was friendly enough that she could have trained anyone, but I did not want that. The last thing I wanted was some pervert asking Ashley to train him as an excuse to stare at her tits. I was happy to help Ashley's dreams come true, but I continued to feel guilty knowing that I bought the gym for all the wrong reasons.

This led me to the most conflictive situation that I have ever been in. I did not know what I was going to do. Ashley was the committed and serious woman I knew. I was fully aware that she deserved the world, but I never had feelings like this. Nonetheless, have someone that had me second guess my lifestyle. Was I going to be faithful to the women I love? Alternatively, was I going to maintain the lifestyle that I was used to? Shit.

13

CHAPTER

THE LATE BIRD

Ever since I met Ashley, I have had mixed feelings about my lifestyle. I have always loved juggling different women, meeting new ones at bars, and being a free man. I began to second-guess myself when I considered my age, desire to have a family, and love for Ashley. I have always wanted to be a parent and a better one than my parents were. They were not awful parents; they never hit me. Fuck, they tried to give me the world. The only issue with my father and mother was that they were never present. Before they were locked up, they worked hours in the lab. I would be lucky if I even have to see them before bed. At times, I felt like they chose their job over me. If they loved me as much as they should have, they would not have been caught making ecstasy. They would have made me their number one priority, raised me, and watched me grow. Instead, I was raised by my Abuela and never received the love from a parent that all my friends had growing up. I blamed my parents for the predicament that I had gotten myself into.

Fable Manny was not weak. Yet, I found myself blowing off girls to be alone. There were many times where I found myself crying with my elbows on my knees and my hands to my head. I felt lost. I did not know what my next step was. If I had parents to guide me, I am sure I would not have been in that situation. I knew that I had two options. Would I be the parent that my parents never were to me?

Settle down with one woman and have a family to come home to every night? Alternatively, would I continue the life that I have made for myself, but most importantly, that I was at?

I knew I had to take into account the women that I was seeing. Were they worth it?

Patricia was the girl I lost my virginity to. She has always been the most laid-back chick amongst all the women. Not only was she aware of my lifestyle, but she also supported it. She would tell me about women from Los Angeles trying to make a living but needed an extra push.

Although I never envisioned a long life with Patricia, she was undoubtedly a woman that I would never forget in my entire life. She was the only one who knew how I lived my life.

Lisa was one of the hardest workers I had met long before she met me. She worked long and treacherous hours as a CNA, making almost no money. She was sweet. She was also one of the first women that I was able to help financially. She was hesitant to accept my help at first but then came to terms with it. She had no idea that I would launch her acting career, and I found that extremely attractive about her. Her innocence was the reason that I would never want to leave her.

Kayla was the woman that I initially had the most suspicion about. She was a connection that was made from church. I thought she was going to be stuck-up and too good. I was utterly wrong.

She continued to surprise me throughout our relationship. I even thought that she could be the one I wanted to spend the rest of my life with. All of that disappeared when I caught that bitch flirting with a guy at the bar. I do not think I ever fully forgave her for all the shit she put me through internally. I never understood what it was about Kayla, but I never seemed able to let her go.

I thought that an excellent way to get back at Kayla was to talk to her cousin, Maya. Maya made it clear that she was much better than her cousin in all aspects of life was. I blew off Kayla several times to see Maya instead. She was sexier and more ambitious. However, she made it clear that she was using me for my fame and riches. I know that she had feelings for me, but she would have done whatever it took to be seen on the front page of every magazine. She succeeded in everything she attempted, and she was worth investing my time into.

I would consider myself the jealous type. I don't particularly appreciate sharing my women with anybody. I know it might sound like I am a hypocrite because I talk to many girls, but I do not think of it like that. I invest time and effort into making the lives of all the girls I get with better.

I guess my jealousy made it a surprise to everyone when I started seeing Elena, who was a stripper. Strippers not only have a terrible reputation, but I also had to deal with many other men looking at my women in the most intimate way. It was different with Elena because she made a career out of stripping and made bank doing it. None of the other women I was with was making the amount of money she was. Our relationship was very business-oriented; she had the money but did not show for it. We worked together to invest the money she has earned. Just as one would expect, she left me. Nevertheless, not for an older and more wealthy man. She left me for a young loser who had nothing to offer her. He ended up wiping her out of all her money, and I was the one who had to clean up after the mess.

Then there was Amy, my high school sweetheart. I do not know if I would consider it love, but I know she did. She left the army and her fiancé to be with me. Although it was a grand gesture, I could not help but think she was somewhat obsessed with our past. What we had was great and fun, but I do not believe she ever could move on. I believe that Amy is the least to expect that I have many girls that I talk to. She has always thought of me as the perfect human, but I am far from that. Amy has held onto the idea of who I was in high school, but I have grown and am a much different person.

Lastly, there was Ashley. She turned my world upside down. She had me reconsider every decision I have ever made. Not only was she the sexiest out of all the women, but she also made me a better man. I wanted her to be the mother of my children. She was the whole package and did not have a single flaw. She did something that no other woman has ever done; she had me second-guessing my lifestyle and wondering if I should drop every other woman to be with her. She cared for me without wanting anything in return. She is the woman that every man dreams of. She has caused the confusion and problematic situation that I am in.

I kept asking myself over and over what I was going to do. I felt like I needed a sign. I felt like I needed my parents. I had the angel on one of my shoulders telling me that I could live the happiest life with Ashley and raise a big family together. However, the devil spoke on my other shoulder and said that I could live the best of both worlds if I continue my lifestyle without change. The devil spoke louder as I realized that I could have cake and eat it too. I was living the life that every man dreamed of. Why would I give up all my women and my lifestyle if I were happy and prosperous?

14

CHAPTER

SELF-CONTROL:
MAYA'S POV

Chapter 14 | Self-Control
Maya's Point of View

My cousin Kayla was right about Fable Manny. He did everything in his power to help launch my career. I went from nobody to being stopped in the streets for photos. I made my first appearance on a television show and my first significant role in a movie. My agent told me that directors have been calling her nonstop with movie opportunities for me. I was being compared to Halle Berry. Everyone loved me. This was a lifestyle that I could get used to.

I was finally able to travel the world, a lifelong dream of mine. I visited a different country every week for interviews, movie shootings, or just for fun. I did not have as much free time as I used to, but I did not mind. I learned that I had to take advantage of the little spare time that I had. I lived life to the fullest with every opportunity granted to me. I partied, did drugs, drank, and slept around. Even though Fable Manny and I were in a relationship, I did not see him enough to be faithful to him.

On a trip to California to visit some friends, I made a shocking discovery. I recently finished shooting my second movie, and as a gift to myself, I decided to fly across the country to have some fun. My friends and I decided to go to a club on my first night in Los Angeles.

We all got dressed to the nines and wore our most expensive clothing. My outfit alone cost more than six figures. My women and I looked fire as we made our way to the club.

I felt all eyes on us when we walked through the double doors, passed the bouncer, and straight into the smoke-filled room with neon lights.

After a couple of drinks, I was ready to dance. I made my way to the dance floor that was already covered with alcohol. Many people, both men, and women tried to dance with me. Nevertheless, my standards were high, and I would not let any loser dance with me. I had an image to uphold, and I knew that paparazzi could be lurking anywhere. The last thing I would want is to be seen on the front cover of a magazine with someone who could not keep up with me. It was not until a beautiful and confident woman came up and started dancing behind me. I shook my ass in her direction, letting her know that I was interested. We continued to dance to the beat of the loud music at the club until she whispered in my ear to go home with her.

One thing I liked about hooking up with females is that they have zero expectations for you after. It's just for fun, unlike men who kick you either out after sex or won't stop calling for a week. The mysterious woman from the club and I walked back to her condominium.

The night was warm, unlike New York, where it was cold the majority of the time. The walk from the club was less than ten minutes, and the next thing I knew, I was having sex with a stranger.

My lifestyle has changed dramatically since becoming famous. This was obvious when the stranger said, "Never did I think I would be running into Maya tonight." She knew who I was, but I did not even know her name. She introduced herself as Patricia. She was a talker as she went on to tell me about her work, party experiences, and other things that I did not remember since I zoned out. When I told her I was originally from New York, she told me one of her business partners is from there too, Fable Manny.

I probably looked like I saw a ghost. How could I tell the woman I just had sex with that Fable Manny was my boyfriend? My silence must have been too long when Patricia said, "Oh. You know him, don't you? Don't worry; many women do." I explained how he helped launch my career and that we were dating. Patricia seemed like she would push for answers, so there was no point in lying. To my surprise, Patricia let out a loud laugh and said, "Aren't we all, honey." Instead of responding with words, I furrowed my eyebrows and tilted my head to the side. What Patricia said was shocking. She exposed my boyfriend, Fable Manny. She knew all of his secrets. That not only he had many girlfriends, but that he was helping launch all of their careers.

I felt confused and did not know precisely how to respond. Why would I have thought that such a successful man would be faithful to me? I guess I should not be one to judge since I was in bed with another woman. However, I did feel less unique that I was not the only one he saw potential in and was helping.

I decided that I would address what Patricia told me to Fable Manny. I wanted him to know that I knew what he was up to. I planned to go straight to his place as soon as my plane landed. I was wondering if I should be petty and say something along the lines of, "Oh, I met a good friend of yours in L.A., her name was Patricia," or be straight up and tell him what I learned. I decided I would do whatever felt best now.

As I was approaching Fable Manny's place, my heart filled with anger. That was until I pulled up to see that he was in his car about to leave. Another white Benz pulled up with a man that I have never seen driving. He walked over to the passenger side, pulled a girl by her hair that looked about my age, and threw her to the curb. I was shocked. I have never seen someone be so aggressively violent towards a woman. The next thing I knew, Fable Manny was out of his car helping the girl get to her feet. The Benz was gone, so I had a clear view of what was happening.

The girl struggled to get on her feet when Fable Manny picked her up bridal style and carried her into his apartment. That is when it hit me. Fable Manny is just helping girls who need a little extra help. If he had never helped me, I would still be waitressing and living with my parents. My life would have never progressed if it were not for his help. Fuck, he even helped my cousin by helping her with her career. He helped other girls to not only make themselves feel better but to help the women find themselves. That was when I realized that Fable Manny was helping women see themselves, and he was trying to help all of us become well.

15

CHAPTER

DEAD EAR:
LINDA'S POV

Thinking back to how I met Manuel still gives me butterflies. It was the perfect beginning to a complicated love story. I thought I would have found love again after my last relationship. Not only that, but who would want to date the woman who is raising a child? I was not very close to my family, and I only had two close friends. I hardly ever spoke to my parents, but when I did, they would complain about me "not trying hard enough to find a man." I think this was the main reason I did not visit my parents often. They did not understand that I was happy with raising my daughter all on my own. This may have been a foreign concept to my parents because they were married when they were eighteen. You know how Asian parents are. They constantly pressured me to have perfect grades in school, marry young, and start a family. I thought that following their footsteps would have resulted in a better outcome. Instead, I ended up divorced and raising a daughter without much help from anyone. I understood that I came with a lot of baggage, and I became comfortable knowing that it will always be my daughter, Isa, and me, that was, until the incident at the park.

My daughter was playing on the swings while I was sitting on the bench reading my book. I would look up occasionally to check on her or be reassured when I heard her tiny giggles.

My heart dropped when I realized that I had not heard Isa's laugh in minutes, and when I looked up, the swings were empty, and there was no sight of my daughter. I was so interested in my book that it was about five minutes until the last time I checked up on her. I stood up from the park bench and did a 360 trying to find Isabella. I always thought that Isa did not need a second parent. I thought I was enough to raise her on my own and did not need a second pair of eyes to look after her. For the first time in eight years, I started to doubt my beliefs. That was when I noticed a stranger walking hand in hand with my daughter, who had swollen red eyes from crying. I ran up to Isa and gave her the biggest hug. My greatest nightmare almost became a reality. Before I could ask what happened, the man who brought my daughter to me said, "She was crying under a tree. I was running but stopped to help her. She said she was lost and wanted to find her mommy." I picked up Isa and held her on my hip. She was eight years old and perhaps a little too big to be held, but I did not care now. I wanted her as close as possible to me. As I was thanking the man for his kind service, I realized that he was extremely handsome. I would have realized sooner, but I was so worried about my daughter.

Isa's headshot right up when she heard the ice cream truck, acting as if nothing happened. Her sad eyes quickly transitioned into puppy dog eyes. This was her usual tactic to get what she wanted, and it always worked.

I tilted my head to the side as if to say, "Not now, Isa, I am talking to the handsome man that brought you back to me." Before I could say anything, he offered, "How about I buy ice cream for the three of us?" Isa jumped out of my arms and ran towards the ice cream truck. "I'm Manuel, by the way. But my friends call me Fable Manny". I reached my hand out to shake his hand. I smiled and said, "Linda."

We spent the entire day at the park. I thought Manny would have parted ways after he bought us ice cream, but he did not. I enjoyed his company much more than I should have. I did not want the day to end. The sun began to set, and Isa was starting to get tired. After several of Isa's tiny yawns, Manny said his goodbyes to us. I did something that was entirely out of my element and asked for his number before he left. I could hear my parents cheer. Anyone who knew me would have been surprised that I asked a man I was attracted to for his number. I felt a sense of embarrassment for not practicing what I preached, but I needed to continue to get to know Fable Manny. He smiled and held his hand out, waiting for me to place my phone in his hand. I handed it over, and he smiled when he saw my lock screen of Isa. It was a picture of Isa standing in front of a field of sunflowers, and she showed the goofiest smile with her missing front tooth. He spent a couple of seconds looking at the picture before he dialed his digits on my phone.

I spent the entire night thinking about him. I never tried dating after my divorce.

I always thought who would want to date the 28-year-old with an eight-year-old child. I married young since I was pregnant with Isa. It would have been frowned upon in my Asian family to have a child without being married. Therefore, that is what I did and regretted it every day. Many of the actions that I carried out when I was younger were made to please my parents. I caught my ex-husband cheating on me when I was five months pregnant. When I took him back, for the sake of our unborn daughter, I saw him in bed with another woman. That was when I packed my bags and moved to New York. He still keeps in contact with Isa but does not see her much because he lives in Pennsylvania. Although I never forgave him, I cannot deny that he loved his daughter. I have had trust issues ever since. Manny seemed different. I felt comforted around him, and he seemed genuine. Without giving it much thought, I texted him and thanked him again for helping me find Isa at the park. I knew it was code to wait a few days to text a man who just gave you their number, but I did not care. I was too old and mature to be following those silly codes. I was shocked when he responded within seconds. After exchanging a few texts back and forth, we had a date planned for dinner the following week. I have not been on a date in years. My main priority has always been Isa, and I never left her side.

Besides that, I was scared to be vulnerable and have my heart broken again. I wanted to keep my outfit simple for our date. I wore skinny jeans, a gold crop top, and nude pumps. My hair was naturally straight, so I did not have to put much effort into it. The next thing I knew, I was in Fable Manny's Mercedes Benz. I was in utter shock when he pulled out a bouquet of sunflowers from under his seat. He smiled and said, "These are for you. I thought that sunflowers were the best option because of the picture I saw of Isa on your phone with the sunflower field in the background."

I was shocked. I sat silently without knowing how to respond. I was never treated like this, and I never knew a man could pay so much attention to detail. I continued to stare at the flowers when he chuckled and said, "Is everything alright?" I smiled, nodded, and grabbed the flowers from him to put on my lap. He gave me a small side smile, and we were off. He was a man and opened my door when we arrived at the restaurant. The feeling of butterflies felt foreign since I have not felt that way in such a long time. When we ordered our food, he seemed distracted. His phone was constantly ringing, and he pretended as if he did not hear it. I also noticed he was reading text messages off his apple watch for most of the dinner. I tried to ignore it, but when his phone rang for the tenth time while we were eating our meals, I snapped and said, "You should probably get that; it seems like an emergency." "It won't be long, I promise," he said.

Instead of answering the call at the table, he stood up and walked towards the restrooms as I hoped he would hear the conversation. A part of me wanted to sneak behind him to listen to what the conversation was. However, I did not. I remained seated for over ten minutes as my lobster ravioli got cold. He rushed over and apologized several times. I told him not to worry about it, and we continued with our dinner. His phone did not ring at all since his last phone call. I was grateful for this but a little suspicious of who it could have been. I had to remind myself that not all men were like my ex-husband.

Not all men were sneaky and cheated on women. I felt awful that I let my intuition get the best of me. I let my suspicions go and spent the rest of the dinner telling Manny my life story. I told him about my strict parents, having Isa when I was 20 years old, and about my cheating ex-husband. He was a good listener and was compassionate about everything I said. He did not have the chance to tell me much about his life besides his work life. I started to get nervous that he would think I was an arrogant woman who only cared about talking about herself. He seemed like the perfect man, and I hoped things would work out for the two of us. Before the waiter brought over the check, Manny asked for a brownie with ice cream for dessert for Isa. This was when I knew I could not let this mango.

He drove me home and thanked me for joining him for dinner. To let him know that I was interested in seeing him again, I said, "Hopefully, we can do this again, but next time I want to hear more about you." We exchanged a quick kiss, and when I reached for the dessert that he ordered for Isa in his Benz, I mistakenly grabbed a woman's heel that was under his seat. He did not see that I saw the other woman's shoe, so I grabbed the box and exited his car. The second I got into my house, my heart dropped. I had a million questions running through my head. What was a woman's shoe doing in his car? Why was there only one? Why was it under the passenger seat? Not wanting it to ruin the magical night I just had, I got in bed and decided to worry about the red shoe another day. I woke up the following day and jumped to my phone, wishing that Fable Manny texted me back. When I checked my phone, there was nothing from him. Only three text messages from my ex-husband reminded me that he would pick up Isa at noon. As much as I hated that man for what he did to me, he tried to be a good father. He drove six hours to New York once a month to spend a weekend with his daughter. My morning was busy as I helped Isa pack; before I knew it, her dad was honking. I gave Isa the biggest hug and sent her off for the weekend.

I threw myself on the couch and checked my phone for what felt like the hundredth time to check for a text from Manny. Nothing. I decided to spend my time looking into Manny on the internet. A part of me felt ashamed for acting like a teenage girl who looked for information online. I felt like I had no other choice. I was bound to find some information on him online; he seemed like he knew many people based on the number of calls he was getting on our date. When I googled his name, many handsome pictures of him popped up. I stopped my investigation to admire how good-looking he was. It was almost too hard to believe. I continued my journey as I scrolled through a few more photos and tried not to get lost in his handsome smile. As I continued digging, I found his Instagram page. His page was mainly selfies and music-related posts. No sign of a secret family or a marriage he was covering up. Was I overthinking it? Was the woman's shoe in his car just an item from his past?

I decided to try one more social media platform, Facebook. His Facebook was dry; it did not get much use. His relationship status said "single," and I felt a wave of relief. I continued to scroll down his page, and I saw a picture of a woman smiling with her face way too close to the man I was falling for. I immediately felt jealous and angry when I saw the caption was a heart emoji. The picture was posted less than a month ago, and I felt like I needed an explanation.

I added the girl on Facebook, and within seconds, she accepted my friend request. My heart plummeted when her profile was flooded with pictures of the man I was falling for with another woman. The poor woman looked so happy; she must not have known that Manny was just as bad as the rest of them.

I did not know what to do. I was shocked. I truly believed Manny was different. Without knowing what my next step was, I put my phone down and cried. This lasted for about an hour before I decided to keep looking into Fable Manny. I went back to Instagram and decided to look into his tagged pictures. I was in total disbelief when I saw that multiple girls were posting pictures with Manny. The pictures made it evident that they were more than friends were. The girls were either kissing him, holding his hand, or had a cheesy caption. How did he get so far with fooling all of these poor, innocent girls? Did they all have zero suspicion that he was seeing multiple women? My heart felt like it was in a knot. I was more shocked at this situation than when I found my husband cheating on me. Manny made it seem like he genuinely cared and that I was the only one. Anger flooded over me when I found myself forming a group chat with all of the girls who posted pictures with him. The next thing I knew, I was inviting them out to dinner the following night. I wanted to waste no time and reveal the truth to all the women who the greatest actor was playing on earth. They were all going to find out who the faithful Fable Manny was.

16

CHAPTER

BEHIND THE
WALLS:
LINDA'S POV

Chapter 16 | Behind the Walls
Linda's Point of View

I planned to embarrass Fable Manny for the cheating,
lying son a bitch that he was. I felt like my actions were
pity, but I did not care. I did feel bad for the girls,
though. They had no idea about the news that they were
going to hear. Surprisingly, they all agreed to meet at the
restaurant at nine that night, and my plan was going
perfectly. Lastly, I texted Manny and told him I had
"great news" to say to him. He pretended to be excited
about my news and agreed to be at the restaurant at nine.
He had no clue that all of the women he was leading on
would also be there.
I felt like I should be the star of a reality television show.
My life has never been filled with so much drama, hatred,
and hurt. I wanted to look my best that night. I liked the
world to see me as the sexy, independent woman I knew I
was. Unlike my first date with Manny, I was no longer
trying to be modest. I wore a tight dress, curled my hair
(which I rarely ever did), and wore a pair of red heels, just
like the shoe I saw in his car. I wanted to look the best out
of all the women he was dating; that way, he would never
forget me. I would be lying if I were not secretly hoping
that he would choose me from all the women.

Although we knew each other for the shortest time, I felt like we had a genuine connection. However, now I was mad. I did not want to hope for an unrealistic future with a cheating man. Isn't being cheated on once enough for a lifetime?

I felt ashamed that I was tricked more than once into trusting and believing a man if I have learned anything from my past, once a cheater, always a cheater.

All the girls agreed to meet at the restaurant at 9 P.M.; they had no idea what to expect. I messaged them and said that I had "life-changing news." I was surprised that none of them asked any follow-up questions. It was as if they knew what to expect, which was impossible. I could have been a serial killer for all they knew. Chances were, they saw my profile picture and thought I was a quiet Asian woman who could not hurt a fly. Little did they know that the news I would deliver would hurt much more than anything they had ever experienced. I was the only oriental woman out of the bunch. However, there was a great variety between skin tones and hair color. Fable Manny did not have a type. My heart went out to the women who expected to have a lifelong future with Manny, as I did. All of their hopes and dreams would have to be recreated with another man once they found out the truth.

Manny picked me up at 8:45 P.M. It may seem immature, but I wanted to show up with him by my side.

I wanted it to be the last time he ever picked up a female while knowing he was leading on multiple women. In addition, I wanted to see the look on all of the other girls' faces.

I wanted them to feel what it felt like when I found their posts on my internet stalking. I felt heartbroken from a man that I only knew within a couple of weeks. It felt like there was no hope for my future in finding love. The woman who was once carefree and happy to live without a man became the opposite of who she always dreaded to be. Manny was keeping up with the entire act. He opened the car door for me and gave me a soft kiss before I entered his Benz. He talked to me normally, asked how my day went and how I was. It hurt to try to talk to Manny as if nothing was wrong. I was shocked that the man beside me tricked so many other women into thinking he was faithful to them. I was holding back tears as I pretended that nothing was wrong. I had to try to be as good an actor as he was. Every time I felt a tear, I played it off like a cough. When we pulled up into the restaurant, my stomach felt like it was sinking into my feet. It was time to show everyone who Fable Manny indeed was.

I was first to walk into the private room of all the women. I almost felt embarrassed for them, even though I was one of them. I walked in with my head facing down, but I noticed that they were all chatting and drinking the moment I looked up.

They even appeared to have already eaten dinner since they all had empty plates in front of them with only scraps of food remaining.

They talked as if they had known each other before that day. They shared laughs, sat very close, and a few women even had each other's hands on one another's shoulder. I thought that it had to have been a mistake. Did I tell them earlier by mistake, and did they all get drunk while waiting for the "life-changing news?" There did not seem to be alcohol in sight, and I was sure I told all the women at 9 P.M. I reread the messages that I sent to them several times. I made sure I was thorough and accurate because I wanted the plan to go smoothly.

I thought I could not have been more shocked. I felt invisible as the women continued to talk as I stood there. What took me off guard was when Manny walked in from behind me. I thought the women would have been confused or angry; instead, they all greeted him. One woman even blew him a kiss from her seat. "We were all waiting for you, darling," one woman said while standing up from her chair. They all seemed genuinely happy to see him. I waited for a few moments to see if they realized they were all drooling over the same man. After two women greeted him with a kiss and no one reacted, I knew I had to step in. "Do you all see what's going on?" I stated the obvious, "You are ALL dating Fable Manny!" The room went silent for a few seconds. Suddenly, everyone burst out laughing.

Not knowing how to react, I remained silent. This felt like a moment out of a nightmare. If this were a reality show, I am sure it would be the most-watched show there ever was because I had never been more shocked in my life. Manny turned to me and said, "You thought you were going to expose me? My ladies all know about each other and accept me for who I am." Manny sat down at the table with the women, and I felt embarrassed. I thought I was doing everyone a favor by the act of kindness I was proving. Instead, I was the fool.

"What the hell is going on?" I yelled. Manny tilted his head to the side, shocked by my sudden burst of anger. "Listen, honey; I told all of my women about the others after a few dates. I would've told you if you didn't try to put me in front of everyone." I shook my head, thinking that what I was hearing was not the truth. Manny deserved an award for best actor because I have never been so fooled in my entire life. He continued to explain that he planned to tell me on our following date, but I did not believe a single word that came out of his mouth. Regardless, what was I supposed to do? Should I be with a man who dates several other women? Manny explained that their relationships were beneficial in every aspect. I could not wrap my head around it.

Before I had a chance to speak, he answered my next question. "And I love every single one of them." All of the women smiled behind him. "Do you all fall for this bullshit? You have to be kidding me. This is sick." A handful of the women stood up from their seats, looking as if they were ready to attack. Manny raised his hand, and the women sat back in their seats. I was disgusted. Fable Manny was essentially a zookeeper, and the women were his obedient animals. I threw my hands up in defeat and walked out of the restaurant with all of the new information. The last thing I heard was the giggles of hopeless women and the sound of Manny's voice.